In Morgan's shadow

Morgan Squa

In Morgan's Shadow

A Hub City Murder Mystery

2001

ISBN 1-891885-25-1
First printing, May 2001

Hub City editor—Betsy Wakefield Teter
Book and cover designs—Mark Olencki
Front cover, back cover and title page images—©2001 Mark Olencki
Author photographs—©1998, 2001 Mark Olencki
Family support—Diana, Weston, Dave, Percy Sox and Sweety
Proofreaders—Laura Corbin and Christina Smith
Canine companions—Ellie Mae and Toby

Hub City Writers Project
Post Office Box 8421
Spartanburg, South Carolina 29305
(864) 577-9349 • fax (864) 577-0188 • www.hubcity.org

Introduction

This is not your average mystery novel.
Call it Extreme Fiction Writing.

Originally written as serial for the Internet, *In Morgan's Shadow* was penned on the fly during a twenty-week period in late 2000 and early 2001 by ten very talented Spartanburg fiction writers with ten very different styles. One would write a chapter, then pass the narrative on to the next author. Each Monday, a chapter was posted on a web site operated by the Spartanburg *Herald-Journal*.

The rules were simple: you had one week to write your chapter, and there would be no discussion about what happens next, especially "who done it." That made for some highly unusual plot twists—and a heap of explaining to do by the last authors in the chain. The writers seemed to be challenging each other to be as creative as humanly possible. "Top this," they said to each other, week after week.

What emerged was a bizarre and lovable cast of characters (some based, not so subtly, on familiar Spartanburg residents) who carried this story from downtown Spartanburg to Landrum to Gaffney and back. Along the way, they visited a host of local businesses, institutions and eateries and, from time to time, poked fun at our way of life here in the Piedmont of South Carolina.

As the mystery deepened, the suspects in the murder of a much-beloved local celebrity multiplied. Was it the enigmatic redheaded Lynn? Was it the driver of that ubiquitous lavender VW Bug? Was it the beloved village idiot savant, Chester? And why on earth had the women of the town taken to the woods in a strange bonding ritual?

This ten-pack of Hub City Writers has woven a wild, unforgettable tale. But perhaps what's most interesting about this book is the variety of writing styles on display here: the comedic touches of John Lane and Sam Howie; the dreamy symphony of words of Rosa Shand; the intensity of language of Thomas McConnell; the mystery-writing prowess of Meg Barnhouse; the wacky mind of Bubba Pat Jobe. There's not a false step anywhere, thanks to the rest of the crew: Deno Trakas (in his fifth Hub City appearance), Norman Powers, Susan Beckham Jackson, and Hub City newcomer Rob Brown.

Thanks go to Andy Rhinehart and Carl Beck of the Spartanburg *Herald-Journal* who commissioned this madcap mystery. And as always, thanks to Hub City's design guru, Mark Olencki, who created the book you are holding.

Let the adventure begin.

Betsy Wakefield Teter
Hub City Writers Project
February 2001

Chapter One

The pigeons swept over Spartanburg. They hovered like wind-caught confetti above the tarnished statue of Daniel Morgan, then settled in the flower beds of the quiet Saturday square. It was the weekend and there would be no city workers in their green and gray work clothes up early before the heat, ambling among the idle sprinklers, looking for the wrappers of Little Debbie cakes tossed from the passing cars. Only a few people would be out this early July Saturday. Maybe, Preston Earley thought as he sipped his coffee from The Sandwich Factory, that's a good thing.

Maybe no one would think him odd as he paused for more than a moment before climbing into his pickup truck, popping it into gear and heading for Dara Flemming's boat house at Lake Lure.

Preston lived in an apartment over the florist shop. His two front windows looked out over the square, past the battered Bradford pears, and from the windows he could take in the downtown. On a clear day he could see the mountains, thirty miles to the north. He liked to stand at the windows and gaze out over the block of grass and vacant parking in the center of town. He and his friends downtown called it "the void," left open after a revitalization project fell through two decades before. The best-laid plans of developers, politicians and bureaucrats had left Spartanburg more than once with such a void at its center. This one they had named "Opportunity Block" with no irony.

As Preston had walked from the coffee house to his truck what had caught his eye was the window, half-open, in the Palmetto Building across the square. Why was that single window open after one of the hottest nights of the Piedmont summer? It had been closed the night before when he had left R.J. Rockers at midnight. Preston was observant. He was no Sherlock Holmes, but he never would have missed an open window on the top tier of two rows of closed windows. Thinking back to his short walk home from Rockers, he remembered looking at the bank of windows in the Palmetto Building. It was well after midnight, and he heard what he thought were fireworks, a sharp pop, pop, pop, and turned to look. Preston would have noticed an open window.

Maybe the apartment dweller was catching an early morning breeze. How likely was that? Preston knew the building was air-conditioned. "Air conditioning," he thought. "Without it, the only thing standing between a Spartanburg summer and hell is a screen door."

Preston noticed things like windows open when they should not be. Hadn't he worked years as a private investigator in Spartanburg? Sure, most of his clients were wives looking for cheating-heart husbands, or more recently a husband wondering where his wife was spending every single evening. He'd not needed many Sherlock skills to solve that mystery. He'd trailed the man's wife up Highway 221 and sat two evenings for hours as she played video poker at the state line parlors.

"You mean there's no man involved?" The disappointed husband had replied when Preston turned in his report.

"You lost her to a poker machine," the detective had replied. "She'll have to come on home once they close 'em down in July."

Now it was July. SLED had been out cruising all the old back-road parlors, and it appeared the state was now clean of its new-found affliction. Preston never quite understood the backlash against what he saw as one of minor sins, gambling. Pride, wrath, envy, lust, gluttony, avarice, sloth. There were the seven deadly sins, and he didn't see video poker anywhere among them.

Preston sipped his coffee and paused one more moment to look at the open window. Was it induction or deduction that Sherlock Holmes used to solve his mysteries? Preston couldn't remember. A window is a window is a window, he thought, slipping into the driver's seat of his truck. Next stop, Lake Lure and the cool waters of Dara's mountain retreat.

Not so fast, Big Guy, Preston said to himself as he drove past the clock tower and looked right down Spring Street. Out of the corner of his eye he saw Crazy Chester twirling down past the Substance Abuse office behind Magnolia Street. He was smiling, staring straight up, trailing what looked like those little triangle flags you used to see flying over used car lots. He flapped his arms in the early heat like a big buzzard trying to take flight. Chester's half crazy and the other half wants to join up, Preston thought. Half crazy, but if anyone was up all night, it would have been Chester. Maybe he knows something.

"Chester," Preston yelled, stopping in the street and rolling down his passenger-side window in the truck. "You hear anything strange last night down near the Palmetto Building?"

Chester continued to twirl. "Depends on whether you gonna buy me a muffin or not."

Preston kept an ashtray full of quarters to feed to Chester like a vending machine. He thumbed out eight and passed them through the open window.

It was always good to keep your sources fat and happy. "Low fat this time."

Chester gripped the quarters in his right hand. He spun like a top. Gun shots," he said. "Twelve fifty seven a.m. Three gun shot."

"I thought it was fireworks," Preston said.

"Most people think it's fireworks, but Chester knows."

"Gun shots on Morgan Square on a Friday night? Why didn't someone report it to the police?"

"Maybe they dumb like you and think it's fireworks."

"I know a gun when I hear one. Eight more quarters if you can prove it. You can have a double muffin morning."

"This proof enough?" Chester pulled three spent cartridges out of his pocket.

"A .38," Preston said. He put them to his nose. "Not fired that long ago."

"Maybe you'll believe me now. Where are those quarters?"

"Okay, Chester," Preston said, counting out four more quarters. "How about seeing what you can find out today? I'll get back by evening."

"So you going to leave this mystery to Spartanburg's finest?"

"Enjoy your muffins, Chester."

"Two big blueberry muffins," Chester said, spinning toward The Sandwich Factory.

Chapter Two

Preston knew the hallucinogens he had taken in Vietnam still affected him, especially when the little man would run down the stem of his glasses and perch on the bridge of his nose. He never took instructions from the little man and soon he'd leave, but Preston also suspected that every voice he heard might not be the result of bad drugs.

He felt marginal on the talking sidewalks and salt and pepper shakers in The Sandwich Factory on Morgan Square. Those voices could have been drugs, disembodied spirits, or aliens operating transmitters from nearby ships hovering over the Spartanburg skyline. But there was no doubt about the statue of Daniel Morgan that guards the square in stony silence.

His voice was the old general himself.

"Solving this one's gonna be trickier than taking pictures of boyfriends and girlfriends across motel parking lots," the old general said, as Preston pretended to be reading the morning's edition of the Spartanburg *Herald-Journal* while leaning against the base of the statue.

"Solving what?" Preston mumbled from behind the paper so the rare Saturday morning passerby would not notice his dialogue with the general.

"The big murder, biggest murder this town has seen in a long time," the general said.

"Maybe some drunk was just target practicing in the Palmetto Building last night," Preston argued and turned the page.

"So you delayed your trip to Lake Lure and the arms of your lady love to hang out and see what happens around some drunk's target practice?" the general replied, and Preston snapped his paper shut and started across the square toward the Palmetto Building.

Maybe in the normal jingle jangle of a weekday, Preston would have been jabbering with the locals on the sidewalk, but in the still, hot, July Saturday morning, he found himself slightly unnerved by the silence and the stillness on the sidewalk in front of the ancient three-story facade.

"You're out of your league, skinny legs," the sidewalk said as he checked the front door.

"Yeah, and you've got grass in your cracks," he

muttered back to the chatty slab.

The wooden stairs creaked under his feet, and dust angels practiced their scales along the edges of the stairwell. He wished somebody would play the radio and drown out all the music from the other side.

He fingered his cell phone from his pocket and called, "Dara, I'm gonna be late. I think somebody's been shot."

"You think?" she oozed in her Bloody Mary drawl.

"I've got three spent cartridges in my pocket, and Chester's pretty sure he heard the shooting just after midnight."

He cleared the second floor landing and saw a pile of furniture through an open doorway.

"Chester's pretty sure they faked Desert Storm, too," she groaned and felt her time with Preston on the lake evaporating.

"I heard the shots, too," he said flatly.

"And you didn't call the boys in blue?" She didn't whine. Dara never whined.

"I love you, baby. I'll call you back."

The pile of furniture beat all.

He had a hard time adding it up.

School desks?

Bookshelves?

Lab tables?

From floor to ceiling?

He remembered that Dawkins Middle School had offered charities in town their old furniture when the new school went up, but what was it doing here among the apartments and offices on the second floor of the Palmetto Building? And who had gone to the trouble of piling it like a bonfire ready to burn?

The room held little else. A ceiling fan twisted like the hands on a cartoon clock. Magazines were stacked next to a worn, dusty-blue recliner, and he spotted a letter, an envelope, both scrawled with that rarest of human expressions, handwriting. The papers scooted in the fan wind.

He picked them from the floor. Only the name "Lynn" was on the front of the envelope, only a brief note was on the single sheet that lay nearby. "Sweetheart, you're a dumb sack of crap. We coulda had it all," and it was signed, "Yer used to be."

Then he saw the blood, and he knew whoever had stopped those .38s was in that bonfire stack of furniture. He sniffed for gasoline and looked around for a pile of soaked rags, but no, the job must have been interrupted.

He slipped the envelope and letter into a copy of *Newsweek* with Bill Gates on the cover and rolled the magazine into the hip pocket of his jeans.

Maybe it was related. Maybe not.

He knew he had to punch in 911 on his cell phone, but a few more minutes wouldn't hurt.

He looked from the still-open window to the street below and wondered if Chester had foundered yet on those two muffins.

He sighed as he reached up and grabbed a student desk off the top of the pile. Whoever had built this funeral pyre was either a strong man or a big-old Roebuck woman.

He knew the cops would squeal over a corrupted crime scene. Maybe he could rebuild the pile after he saw the stiff. The general's warning about a "big murder" was just too much juice for a P.I. unaccustomed to the big time.

Pulling one lab table away from the tangled mess, he saw hair, and leaning in he could see the side of the face. Definitely of the male persuasion, he mused.

Holy catfish.

Not that any of them don't, but this one would definitely make the papers. Preston started to call his old buddy, Barry Skidwitch, so he could start writing the half-acre of newsprint this baby was gonna take.

Instead he just dragged down a big breath and savored the moment. Cops would be here soon enough, reporters not far behind. Son of a…

Phil Quake, the earthquake morning man of Spartanburg radio, lay dead as a hammer under piles of surplus school furniture.

Preston couldn't help but lean forward and listen to the sound of silence.

Chapter Three

It had been three weeks. Three weeks of finding out nothing and going nowhere quick. Phil Quake was dead, and the aftershocks of his murder were still being felt. After another look at the corpse and intensive peering into every nook and cranny of the room, Preston had finally called the cops. There had been a few questions to answer, but Preston had enough of a decent reputation with the local police that he'd gotten away with only a lecture on the dangers of impeding an investigation.

"You sure you didn't touch anything but the furniture, Earley?"

Preston looked at his old friend, Lieutenant Bo Hunter of the Spartanburg Department of Public Safety. "Bo, I'm not a rookie. Yeah, I moved furniture. But when I found the body, I set everything back in place and called 911."

"I believe you, but I gotta ask. And Chester, he gave you the .38 shells and came up with the time?"

"Yeah. Last I saw he was on Spring Street."

"Got it. Thanks for the call, Preston. It's gonna be wild when this gets out."

Lieutenant Hunter's comment had been the height of understatement. Wild hadn't even begun to describe the uproar. The first that most of Spartanburg knew of the events of early a.m. Saturday were when they opened their papers on Sunday morning. There, splashed across the front page in World War III Elvis Is Dead typeface, was the headline: Phil Quake Murdered!

The response had been overwhelming. No one could name a resident of Spartanburg more loved than Phil Quake. Every charity in town, every good cause that got too little attention or was underfunded had been a recipient of his help. Now, people wanted an answer.

The turnout for Quake's funeral rivaled that for British royalty, and seating inside the church had been at a premium. Politicians, local and area dignitaries, business people, and a wide cross section of folks from the entertainment industry were scattered throughout the crowd. Strom Thurmond was squeezed in between John Boy and Billy, while Jane Robelot was actually perched on Lou Holtz's knee. Jane looked uncomfortable, but Lou didn't seem to mind.

In the days that followed, theory after theory about the case was put forward, but nothing made sense. Preston was following the case in the paper and asking a few discreet questions on the street, but even the ever-reliable Chester seemed baffled by the murder. He could only offer up half-baked opinions on FBI involvement and black helicopters, in exchange for Preston's quarters. The only thing noteworthy had been where Chester found the shell casings—on the ground beside the passenger door of a lavender 1966 VW Beetle parked across from Java Jive. He found the casings at 1:03 a.m. Just six minutes after he heard the shots. Chester had shared this with the police as well, so Preston was on the same page when he met Bo Hunter at Papa Sam's for breakfast.

"Morning, Preston. Been peeping into any motel windows lately?"

"A few, Bo. How about you, still doing all your police work from a stool at the Krispy Kreme?"

They laughed at one another and placed their orders. "I'll have a cup of coffee and whole wheat toast, no butter," said Preston.

"You know, Preston, eating like that can't be good for you," said Bo. He grinned up at the waitress. "I'll have a trashcan omelet, a side of bacon, a side of sausage, homefries, toast with extra butter and a Diet Coke."

The waitress smiled and winked. "You tryin' to loose weight again, Bo?"

"No darlin', just doing what it takes to maintain this fine crime-fighting physique." The waitress rolled her eyes and went to place the order.

"Okay, Bo, what's the problem? Three weeks and no answers. Do you even have a suspect?"

Bo looked casually around to make sure no one could overhear. "No suspect, no motive, no nothing. We're at a dead end." They paused while the waitress put down their water and Diet Coke.

Preston looked into Bo's eyes. He had never seen his old Army buddy quite so pensive. Reaching into his pocket, Preston took out a small pill case and popped a tablet into his mouth.

Bo looked concerned. "Having trouble again, Preston?"

"Just a little. Had an episode the day I found Quake. Doctor tells me I'll be fine as long as I stay on my meds."

"Good, can't have you freaking out on me just when I need your help."

"What have you got?"

"Not much. Phil had no enemies and no one who would benefit from his death. The information from Chester about the time he heard the shots and the time he found the shell casings are the only thing we've got to even pinpoint the time of death. The coroner agrees within an hour on either side of 1 a.m., but that's it. No witnesses and no fingerprints at the crime scene—except yours."

"Am I a suspect?"

Bo flashed a grim smile. "I wish. Then I could just cuff you after breakfast and take you in."

"Why after breakfast?"

"That's in case you're buying."

"Not much of a chance on that. What else have you got?"

Bo reached into his shirt pocket, took out two folded sheets of paper, and handed one of them to Preston. "This is a list of everything on Phil Quake's body. Somewhere on the list is a clue. Maybe several."

Preston read down the list. Wallet (brown leather tri-fold), South Carolina driver's license, Social Security card, expired hunting license, watch (Timex), thirteen Sacagawea gold dollars, and a claim check from Dunbar's Gun Shop.

"No pictures?"

Bo looked around again before handing Preston the second sheet of paper. Preston unfolded it and looked at a color copy of a young woman. Staring up at Preston was the face of a beautiful redhead. Across the photo was written, "All My Love—Forever and More, Lynn."

Both the dazzling beauty of the woman and also her apparent youth stunned Preston. Phil Quake was in the neighborhood of sixty. The woman was maybe pushing twenty.

"Think this is the same Lynn from the note in the apartment?"

Bo nodded. "Maybe, but the handwriting on the note doesn't match Quake's, and it doesn't match the handwriting on the photo. I've floated copies of the picture among the usual informants, but so far no one has any idea who she is."

Preston thought a moment. "What about the rest of the stuff? This claim check from Dunbar's. It isn't on a possible murder weapon, is it? Say, a .38 caliber pistol?"

Bo leaned across the table and grinned. "You know, I wasn't really sure how much investigating you had done in that apartment before we arrived."

"What do you mean?"

"Preston, you obviously didn't move the body. If you had, you would have known."

"Known what?"

"The one thing we've not let out to the public."

Bo reached back into his pocket and pulled out a crime-scene photograph, which he slid upside down across the table to Preston.

Preston turned the picture over and gazed in stunned amazement at the gruesome photo.

Chapter Four

"So, now you see why we want to keep this quiet as long as we can," Bo said, dousing ketchup on his omelet.

Preston swallowed to force back the bitter taste coming up his throat. "You and I both know the bullet wounds look like the least part of this desecration," he said, trying not to look at Bo licking ketchup off his finger.

"Yeah, well, you're right, of course. At least we do know a .38 snub-nose police special fired the bullets, same as the gun make on the claim check. But that doesn't tell us what all the other is about."

Preston stood up. He couldn't look at any more food and wondered how even Bo, steel stomach and all, could eat after the picture they'd just studied. He'd like to forget about this murder. But he couldn't. Not the least reason being that the radio station had put him on retainer now. What with three weeks gone by and the police finding nothing.

Standing outside Papa Sam's, Preston felt woozy. Swimmy-headed like he always felt before the voices came. He needed to get somewhere quiet and think some pleasant thoughts.

He started the short walk back to his apartment. Already, this early in the day, the August heat saturated the air. Spartanburg had been without rain almost since the murder. Even the weeds had stopped growing. At least that was good for Chester. He would get a break from mowing in this searing heat. Poor Chester. Along with whatever handouts came his way, he got by keeping grounds and cleaning gutters.

The accident had happened so many years ago. Chester had been a star senior at Spartanburg High School with scholarship offers for discus throwing from all over the country. Then during a meet with local rival Dorman High, a shot put knocked him senseless and changed everything. The heavy ball careened into the back of his head. For several days, it was uncertain if he'd even recover consciousness. And yet here he was alive and well (in body and spirit if not mind) and seemingly content with life. Maybe, Preston thought, that was better than constantly fearing the voices and flashbacks like he did.

And yet Chester could surprise you sometimes. Like how he found those bullet casings so quickly.

Java Jive was a block over from the murder scene. How had he done that? Could he possibly? No way. But didn't he say, "Chester knows," a voice in Preston's head cut in. "Not going there," Preston said out loud to the phantom trying to encroach on his sanity.

Those pleasant thoughts. Where were they? Dara. Ah, Dara. Now there was one. He imagined her floating—slender, long arms dangling in the water—on her yellow rubber raft at Lake Lure. Keeping cool and waiting for him. But actually, Dara had been home for quite a few days, and he'd hardly seen her. His fault, but he'd just had so much on his mind. He knew she was perturbed, without even checking. So he was putting off calling her. He hated approaching Dara when she was mad. She didn't whine, but she had her ways to cut him off. It'd be better to appease her beforehand.

He turned the corner onto his block and looked toward his apartment. Flowers, of course. Here he lived right above Mrs. Glenn's shop and sending Dara flowers hadn't even occurred to him until he was standing right in front of the sign. The sign just said "Florist." She didn't need a name. Hers was the oldest business downtown. Florence Glenn had been in business since she was a girl, practically. Started making her own living when her young husband was killed in World War II and she was pregnant with their daughter, Patricia.

Why hadn't he thought about talking to Mrs. Glenn about the murder? Between her and her old maid sister and roommate, Lucille, who'd been teaching algebra more than thirty years, they knew just about everyone. Well, he'd see her now and accomplish two things at once. Already he felt better.

The little bell jingled, and cool air splashed him in the face. He drew in a deep, earthy breath of moss and fern.

"Well, hello, neighbor." Mrs. Glenn pulled aside the faded curtain that separated the shop from her workroom. She wore her gray hair coiled in two knots at the back of her head, and her skin was as wrinkled and delicately beautiful as the petals of the carnations in her glass front cooler. It was obvious she had been lovely in youth, but the same could not be said for her sister, Lucille Stone, who trailed her from the workroom.

Miss Lucille had probably never been called beautiful by anyone. Sturdy was probably the kindest word. Except for her round face surrounded by thin, yellow hair frizzing out all over, she was a square block from her fencepost neck down to her thick, solid ankles. "How do, Mr. Earley," she greeted him.

"Hot morning, ladies. Sure does feel good in here. Looks like the flower business is blooming."

"We've been so busy. Been having Lucille in to help me. Good thing the murder happened when school's out, say Lucille?" She looked affectionately toward her sister and smiled. "I'd said to Lucille just the week before it happened, hadn't I, Lucille, that what I needed was one good funeral because business had been so slow. I was starting to get worried. But all this. I wouldn't have wished murder on anyone, least of all Phil. He was our down-the-street neighbor in Converse Heights, for goodness sake."

"Poor Phil," Miss Lucille echoed her sister. "Everybody loved him." The words were right, but her tone sounded a bit disdainful, Preston thought. Ever the thoughtful sleuth, he remembered that once Miss Lucille had been interviewed on the Phil Quake show.

Though the school district loved her, wouldn't let her retire, everyone knew Miss Lucille's ego thrived on something else.

She was an amateur poet. The kind who wrote sentimental hymns and school alma maters. She passed out copies of her verse to bank tellers, gas station attendants, and anybody else she could unload them on. Preston remembered Phil Quake interviewing her when she was named Poet Laureate of the South Carolina Music Federation. Phil, certainly not meaning anything by it other than the truth, said, "Miss Lucille, now that you've been named Poet Laureate of the Music Federation, tell us when you're going to write something new under the sun."

But she apparently hadn't thought his question clever. For several seconds there'd been dead air on the radio. Then music started playing.

"Guess you'll be headed back to the schoolhouse soon," Preston said, shifting from one foot to the other, his thoughts starting to spin, not believing what he was thinking. "Say, you don't know anything about that pile of school furniture found at the murder site do you, Miss Lucille? Since it came from your school and all."

She gave him a hard stare. "Well, I don't know anything except I asked my friend Ed Barnes if he'd let the school store what wasn't donated last year in the basement of his building." Ed was the proprietor of the Palmetto Building.

"Lucille," Mrs. Glenn's voice cut in at a too-high pitch. Preston shifted his gaze and saw Mrs. Glenn's expression before she could recover. Those gentle blue eyes had the look of alarm, no doubt about it.

Crazy? Maybe, Preston thought. He ordered a dozen yellow roses and formulated a plan.

Chapter Five

BY THOMAS McCONNELL

First thing was to hand-deliver this dozen to his own little yellow rose of Texas. That would be just enough calculated corniness to draw a smile from Dara Flemming and give him a cool pause in her good graces to talk this out—she could tell him if he was tracking the right animal. Dara F Lemming. She'd gotten a credit card offer addressed like that once. Credit line to $100,000. Like she needed any more zeros.

"Well. I guess there's nothing to do but head over the cliff," she laughed, as she did at most things.

"Better than over the hill. How about let's go to Acapulco? I'm ready soon as you sign," and he'd danced the form before her eyes.

"Lake's out there if you want to go diving. No, I can't see as how I'd trust you in a country where the dollar was strong as the tequilla."

"Me?"

She didn't bother looking at him. "I want a place a bit more exotic—Phuket all the way," she said. "Thailand." A travel magazine landed spread in his lap, a shining red nail darted at a beach emerald and white and aquamarine.

Hmm. He didn't know about Asia yet, the jungle, and had grown as quiet then as he was now, sitting in his truck in Morgan Square. Some rounded car pinged past and he raised his eyes to the parking lot before him aswim in the heat. The truck cab was sopped in it, yellow petals already crinkled at the edges, he could smell them wilting along with the steamed flower shop moss. His mind began projecting a movie he not only hadn't paid for but had been trying to skip out on for twenty-five years, the first frame Bo Hunter's shaded profile smeared black and green, the ear ochre.

Then the soundtrack began, his mind crunching a word salad no meds could toss. He tried to focus on the statue of Morgan above, to see if squinting into the old man's distant eye might slow his nerves. Sacagawea. Lucky thirteen. Watch (Timex) (still ticking). Expired Social Security card. Lucille-cold-as-Stone. Phil Quake colder still, a desecration, heart on his short sleeve. "You think it was so jolly," the old general's sad face said, "jaunting through the woods in fringed buckskin and this extravagant headdress wondering who could be depended on and who couldn't?

"My arthritis so sharp it felt like somebody was hammering a nail down the marrow of each thumb bone. And my back; don't even let me go there. That's why I quit the war. You know why an old man shuffles? Cause his lower back's all unstrung, I tell ya, loose as old Lucille's flabby upper arm in yonder.

"Weak as your Mr. Phil Quake's sacroiliac. Yeah, you saw him stooped at more than one fundraiser, remember, and it wasn't on account of no too-pink chicken, though there was always plenty of that to go round. Try sitting at a mic for near forty years and see what it does to your lumbar spine. You'd need to grow a hand on your tailbone to help you out the chair. You're missing something, I tell ya."

"What?"

"It's your blind spot. Everybody's got one."

"What?"

"Jacksnipe, don't ask me what. Get out that sheet of paper."

Preston pulled the list of Quake's effects from his back pocket, unfolded it, a quincunx of begrimed holes where the creases intersected.

"What you need is there, but turn it over for now."

"There's nothing on the back."

"Not yet, Pea Eye, but there will be. Get out your handy-dandy detective pencil."

Preston fumbled a green stub courtesy of the

Georgia Lottery off the dash and followed Morgan's orders.

"Mark an X on the paper. Now make a dot about six inches to the right of that. Good. Hold it at arm's length, close your left eye, keep your right on the X, then slowly bring the paper toward you."

The X approached, the dot disappeared. He opened his eye, and there it was again on the page. He put the paper from him again, brought the X near, saw the dot vanish once more from his sight.

"What's that?"

"Your education for today: meet your blind spot. I've been trying to tell ya, you're missing something."

"Do I need to see a doctor?"

"Yes, chucklehead, and the diagnosis is you need to think for a change. Now think. When the SHJ declared that Spartanburg had no resident better loved than P.Q., they didn't know the half of it."

Preston thought: was it induction or deduction? Finally, abjectly, he asked, "What am I missing?"

"Earley, you've got all the penetration of a Neanderthal. Don't ask me what, I just happened by some accident of personal history to have my head turned the wrong way that Saturday midnight, but try this on for size: an old man with a bad back and a young girl—something ain't fittin."

The first drops fell then, cratering the dust on the windshield, the hood. He hadn't even noticed the thunderheads rising to the south. Hallelujah.

Rain. The asphalt sighed its steam as if thankful, and Preston cranked his window down all the way, thrust his own grateful hand cupped into the shower. He left downtown headed north, fancying himself a fugitive outrunning the storm all black in his rearview mirror. The rain paused as he passed under a trestle, beneath the repeated kuhump of a line of hopper cars tagged KILLA! by who-knows-what hand headed who-knows-where. The rain was falling harder when he met it again, and just as he was half wishing it would clot into snow, a downpour came so thick and fast he withdrew his smarting palm, raised the window, his wipers useless. He could no longer see the Wade's Roll Model strutting her risen stuff down the runway of the billboard. A tanker truck flung a whole puddle in his face so he couldn't even see the dealer tag of the car in front of him, the requisite pine-green SUV of a soccer mom who considered it a point of pride to have touched no ball of any description since seventh grade. But the car behind he could detect too well, the glare of its high beams striking off the mirror at his eyes now suddenly groping in this afternoon become twilight. He tried waving the other driver off, flicked the mirror lower, grunted when the car juked out of traffic to overtake him, a 1966 VW Beetle not lavender but the very color of the rain, edging beside him, edging closer to the center line, too road-raging close. There was a car horn, a long wet screech. Then he could see nothing.

Chapter Six

BY ROSA SHAND

He wasn't awake but he heard voices—as if they were coming across some vast and unknown space.

His eyes flickered open and quickly closed.

White—a hospital. People over him—one yanking his finger like the witch in Hansel and Gretel. The voices were far away as ever but the next he knew it was one voice near his face. A woman's. Not Dara's. Low and soothing. Steady, no changing in tone. The voice had been going on some time—he was vaguely aware of that.

When his eyes could open he was flooded with relief and happiness. He was staring in her face. Quite close. He was flooded with relief and happiness. She was beautiful—and he knew her—close to intimately. But he couldn't remember where and why and how.

She was important to him. Holy moly—did he have amnesia?

The storm. The 66 Bug nudging him off the road. Now, the hospital—he did not have amnesia. Hallelujah.

But how did he know this face? No one would forget it. Black eyes—huge, calm. Auburn hair—straight—streaming around her face, drawing him—it might as well be—into the tent of her hair.

He began catching what it was she was saying: "You are safe. You must speak— tell me what is in your mind before you wake up all the way. Talk to me. Tell me…"

Was she hypnotizing him?

Creakily, unsteadily, he came out with sounds. And then he found some kind of voice: "A fire—a strange hillside place, an amphitheater like the one at Converse. But dry country. White rocks. Seats in a circle. At the bottom—one gigantic fire. I swan! It should have been a friggin' nightmare because they were about to burn an old gray man but all of us kept watching—like it was fate. Oh no—now I remember—last night—on television—a weird advertisement I kept thinking about. Bits of a ballet, The Rite of Spring—I recognized it because my ex-wife had the video—wild red figures like cannibals dancing around this fire—it was the feeling I had—exactly—in this dream. I swanie.

"Oh…" He stopped speaking. He knew what he

was dreaming! He recognized the fire—fire had played on the edge of his mind for over a month now—the killers intending to burn Quake (they had to have been scared off—there had to have been a passel of buggers to have raised that pile of lumber over that body—the gun-person had skeedaddled but that scalawag was being used—couldn't be the instigator). Fire and desecration—there was the fascination of abomination—ritual sacrifice! Yeah, sacrifice means burning, you would think—but those prehistoric myth-makers didn't take to logic—couldn't stick to a simple job like burning a victim up—they moved on to ripping a body to pieces. By Jove! That was on Morgan Square—that mutilated body and that pyre! Holy moly, it was all so obvious—like the general warned! These fiendish modern Spartans had passed their Western Culture class, read up on the cult of Dionysus. That was the god of poetry, wasn't it? He had his hopped-up women worshippers, didn't he? —tore his body to pieces—ate his inspiration. Wasn't that it? Call these creatures the Bacchi—some do. Addicted to bacchanals, he heard. But the Bacchi—they were men as well as women if he remembered right.

Okay. But that was the dawn of history. Today it took his dreaming to stumble on rank defilement like this—primitive ritual spank in the middle of the rational upcountry Spartans (skip it that the *Herald-Journalers* tear open the paper to the horoscope and fight for time at the palm readings out on the Chesnee Highway. Never mind those aberrations.) Spartans slam their doors on inspiration. And hallelujah for that—who's gonna cope with inspiration that winds up sacrificing gods? (And who was a god these days but the talk-show media king?)

Yes but. This was a baby step. Now the search: just who were the Spartan Bacchi?

Lucille! She was the single poetess he could muster at the moment. Jiminy Cricket—how could he forget that cabal at The Sandwich Factory?

Cripes—who would he eat breakfast with? Forget accusing that gaggle. Anyway scribbling was not the same as madness. Or was it?

Try Greek connections then. The city wangled its name from Greece somehow. The population groans with Greeks. But shoot—that Greek Church ought to rein in primitive Greeks. Tarnation! He forgot there was that spooky poet at Wofford they didn't seem to muzzle...

* * *

These tedious explanations—of course they'd hit him quickly and confusedly—within seconds of the time his dream had banged that truth through his skull. And he was bound to have been picking up hints before—like the 666 that popped in his mind with the 66 Bugs that were nibbling at this case. Still, when this obviousness struck him he'd closed his eyes at once, stopped talking to this beauty. Though he could feel her leaning over him, keeping up her monotone. He couldn't fathom her aim.

But he knew her! Who was she?

His eyes popped open. He focused intensely on her. She hushed. She didn't turn away. Rather she began to smile at him, intimately, but at the same time not quite intimately. She was also holding her distance—was she trustable? Her eyes had a kind of teasing, a knowingness, as if she somehow meant the two of them were in cahoots.

Abruptly he recognized her. Heavens to Betsy—the redhead in the photograph! And that same instant he grasped he loved this woman—whoever, whatever, she was—in a way that was different from anything he'd met. Ever. This turn of events he had not counted on. But here it was. And all in spite of what he'd be to her, that fact, sadly, he somehow knew already.

What he said was, "Dadgummit, sweetheart—why are you asking me these things?"

She drew back. She said, "I am doing research. In psychiatry. Studying what's in people's minds when people come out of trauma. Do you mind?"

He nodded no. He said, "You know, sweetheart, I am somewhat acquainted with you. You were a buddy of the late Phil Quake."

He took in her shock, her confusedly sweeping her long hair back with her hand.

He said, "You were kinda intimate with him."

Now she laughed. She said, "You say that—it shows you are not acquainted with me at all." She stopped laughing, but she hadn't stopped rather nervously playing with her hair. She said, "He interviewed me once—about this study. After that we kept up what you might call a teasing friendship. I've been devastated by this thing."

"I see. But, then,...still, do you..." he hesitated and then he shot it out, "Do you write poetry, sweetheart?"

Chapter Seven

BY DENO TRAKAS

Earley could tell he'd caught her by surprise again. "Why yes, I dabble a little, poetry and fiction—I've taken some classes at Converse. Why do you ask?"

At the mention of Converse, his mind flashed back to his vision of the outside amphitheater, the fire, the old gray man…it seemed too vivid to be a dream. He was about to ask her, this intimate stranger, what was her name again, Lynn, lovely Lynn, this radiant redhead he loved passionately and inexplicably, he wanted to ask if he could warm his hands in her hair…no, that wasn't it…if she had seen Phil Quake the day of his death, yes, that was it, but before he could speak, Dara swept into the room, carrying a Talbot's bag. She took in the scene, the pretty girl—any female half Dara's age was a girl—

leaning forward over the bed with a tape recorder and legal pad, looking back over her shoulder resentfully at the shopper who had barged in.

Dara, never one to be intimidated, throttled right up to Earley's bed, leaving Lynn in her wake, and said, "Well, well, my dear, I didn't know you were back among the living, much less entertaining coeds." She plopped her bag on the bed beside him and pecked him on his chapped lips.

Lynn rose from her chair, clutching her pad and recorder to her breast with one hand and smoothing her skirt with the other. "Thank you for your help, Mr. Earley."

He wanted to tell her to stay, he had more questions, lots of them, and not just about Phil Quake, the hell with Phil Quake, but he said, "Yeah, sure, my pleasure Miss..." But she was already headed for the door and didn't fill in her name.

Dara began taking things out of her bag—a James Hall novel, a box of granola bars, an eight-pack of strawberry-kiwi V-8 juice, a ten-pack of spearmint gum—and said, "Who was the sweetcheeks?"

"I'm not sure," he said. "But she's the girl in the picture found on Phil Quake when he was murdered."

"Oh? What was she doing here? Was she going to do you, too?"

"Do me?"

"Yeah, do you, ice you, snuff you."

"I wish you'd stop watching the *Sopranos*, darlin'.

But, as a matter of fact, I think someone DID try to kill me."

"What are you talking about?"

"The accident—it was no accident. I was run off the road."

"What?!"

"I can't be sure. The whole thing is still foggy."

"But why? Who'd want to kill you?"

"I don't know, babe. Who would want to kill Phil Quake?"

"What did the bimbette want?"

"She said she was doing research, studying what's in people's minds when they come out of trauma, something like that."

"And you believed her? My God, what if she IS the killer? What if she was here to finish you off, like that scene in *The Godfather*?" Dara began to twist her hands as if she were rubbing Keri lotion into them.

"Now don't get all worked up, darlin'. I'm sure she's legit."

"I want you to call Bo Hunter this instant."

"Now, now." He scooted over, moved the presents she'd brought, and patted the bed beside him. "Come here, babe." She sat, swung her legs up and snuggled into him. He put his arms around her firm body, realizing for the first time that he had an IV stuck into his hand.

"I'm glad you're okay, honey," she said.

"How long was I out?"

"You've been off and on like a shorted lamp for two days. How do you feel?"

"A little woozy. But mostly hungry."

"I brought you some granola bars."

"Thanks, but I want some real food. I feel like a Dionysus burger."

"Why on earth?"

"I don't know. It's like I've been thinking about it for days. And I need to go to the Spice anyway—I've got some questions for Leo and Theo."

"Whatever you want, sugar. As soon as they release you."

"Well, what are we waiting for?" He found the call button and buzzed the nurse.

When they got up to the counter at the Sugar-n-Spice, Leo asked, without looking up from his preparation table, "What'll it be, folks?"

"A Dionysus burger and an order of half and half," Earley said.

"Make that two," Dara added.

Hearing the familiar voices, Leo looked up, and Theo glanced over his shoulder from the grill—both Greek brothers smiled. "Where you been, Preston?" Theo asked.

"I've been on a diet—doctor says my cholesterol's too high."

"You're safe here. You've heard of the Mediterranean diet, haven't you? All Greek food is healthy."

Dara laughed and said, "Right. Like that low-fat,

low-calorie baklava."

"Yes ma'am, best health food in town," Theo said. "Pick up a piece down the line—Mama made it yesterday."

"I think I will. I did an hour on the Stairmaster this morning."

"How come y'all don't put the Dionysus burger on the menu?" Earley asked.

Leo answered, "You're the only one who orders it, outside of family."

"They don't know what they're missing," Earley said. Theo flipped a couple of burgers onto buns, and Leo smothered them with feta cheese, tomatoes, black olives, grilled onions, and a splash of olive oil. It was Earley's favorite food. "Hey, fellas, did y'all know Phil Quake?"

"Sure," Theo said as he added fries and onion rings to their trays. "Ate here every Thursday. Terrible shame."

"Who woulda thought something like that could happen in Spartanburg," Leo wondered aloud as he began the next order.

A line was forming behind them, so Earley knew he couldn't stand there and chitchat, but he said, "You can't think of anyone who'd want him dead, can you?"

"No, not me," Leo said.

"Me either," Theo said. "He was a nice guy. Always did his show from the Greek Festival. Are you investigating, Preston?"

"Yeah. Listen, just one more question. You fellas know anything about rituals that would include human sacrifices, or desecration of bodies, or funeral pyres?"

"What the hell you talking about, Preston? I thought Quake was shot," Leo said.

"Right, he was. This is, um, something else."

"We used to do human sacrifices at Harry's," Theo deadpanned. "They weren't very popular. That's why we sold the place."

"Okay, okay. Thanks...for the burgers, fellas. But if you hear anything out of the ordinary, give me a call."

"Sure thing, Preston. Dara. Come back and see us."

They slid their trays down the counter, picked up a couple of pieces of baklava and a tea and a water, paid Mrs. C, ducked under one of the hanging ferns and settled into a booth. On one side of them were four men dressed in the blue uniforms of Piedmont Natural Gas, and on the other side were a couple of jeans-and-flannel tree-hugging Wofford professors.

"What was that all about?" Dara asked.

"Nothing," Earley mumbled from a mouth full of burger.

"You've got to give up this ridiculous investigation, honey. Let the police handle it."

"I can't, Dara. It's gotten personal."

"But it's been a month and there aren't even any

suspects."

He took a swig of sweet tea and noticed that his sandwich was already gone. He thought about going back for another one, but instead started eyeing Dara's, hoping she'd notice and feel sorry for him. "Well, maybe not, but we've definitely got some leads."

"Like what?"

"Oh, little things." He started shoveling in the fries. "That's what's got me stumped. Daniel Morgan said it was big."

"Daniel Morgan, the Revolutionary War guy?"

"No, of course not," he lied. "An old friend of mine, you don't know him. I just can't figure out how this could be a big story. I mean, what's big in Spartanburg?"

"Well, there's Maud Rellikin, the wealthiest person in South Carolina," she said and took a dainty bite of the burger he coveted.

"Yeah. I hadn't thought of her. I wonder if she knew Phil Quake. They're about the same age. Or were. Whatever."

"And then there's the Renaissance Project."

"Yeah, I hadn't thought of that either. Dadgummit, Dara, you're making my head spin."

"That's never been hard, honey."

Chapter Eight

BY NORMAN POWERS

Dusk was creeping through Spartanburg. Preston stood at his apartment window, watching the square below turn to velvet and the sky fade to burnished silver. He was not normally given to poetic reflection and thought it might have something to do with the two Krispy Kremes he had consumed (the second one just going down, smooth and sweet), washed down with an ice cold can of diet soda. Still, he couldn't help gazing out to the northwest, where the dusky blue mountains were etched against the horizon. Their solitary splendor made murder seem even more of an unnatural act. Too bad they'd put old Daniel so he faced away from them, the mountains eternally lurking just out of the corner of his bronzed and sightless eyes. "Who are you to talk about blind spots, you old geezer," Preston muttered.

"What?" Dara was just locking down his battered old suitcase, stuffed with a week's worth of his clothes for the boathouse at Lake Lure.

"Nothing. Just thinking out loud. About something somebody said to me about a blind spot. Y'know, not being able to see something even though it's right in front of you?"

"I don't want us to get started on all that again, hon. You need a break from this mess, and I'm about to see you get it. No more talk about mutilated bodies and pawnshop tickets, and *especially* about young girls with red hair appearing at your bedside. Ready?"

"I guess." Still, he found it hard taking his eyes off those dark, reassuring mountains, in stark contrast to the fevered light of his dream…the burning light of that fantastic amphitheater, and something else that suddenly burst into his memory of that awful scene. There had been a stone, too, he now remembered. The grotesque, leaping figures had been dancing around a kind of upright stone slab…

"Well?" Dara's voice broke the spell.

Preston meekly followed her down the stairs and out onto the street. Across the square, the yellow police tape over the entrance to the Palmetto Building glowed in the fading light, as if some awful residue of the crime scene upstairs had leaked down through the passageway and onto the street. Old Daniel still resolutely turned his back on the scene of the crime, and this time had nothing to say to Preston. Maybe

Dara had put the fear of God into him.

There was a rustling behind them.

"Chester misses you!" The ragged, squat figure danced up to them out of the gloom.

"Just be away for a week, Chester," Preston assured him. "Dara here's locking me away in her boathouse up there at Lake Lure."

Chester waggled a finger at Dara. "You watch out for him, pretty lady. He's Chester's best friend."

"Mine, too, Chester." Dara smiled.

"You drivin' out on 176?" Chester asked Preston.

"Well…we thought we'd just take Highway 9 all the—"

"That 176 can be a nice road. Lots to see." He sidled closer to Preston and laid a grimy hand on his arm. "Chester remembers the border stone," he whispered.

"What are you talking about, Chester?"

But Chester's eyes had fallen on the box of doughnuts cradled under Preston's arm. "You takin' those Krispy Kremes with you?"

Preston held out box just out of his reach. "What's a border stone?"

"Chester's been there, but nobody saw him." He grabbed the box of doughnuts and stared intently through the cellophane window. "These aren't the low-fat ones, are they?"

Preston tried to switch his mind to Chester's way of seeing the world, and after a moment came up with a translation. "Are you talking about the state line?" Preston wanted to know. "And if you are, how the heck did you get yourself all the way out there and back?"

Dara suddenly stepped closer, peering at Chester. "On the trains. The freight trains that run out that way going up to Asheville. Isn't that right, Chester?"

"The border stone can tell you things. Chester knows." He shoved the doughnuts under his arm and wandered off, his long cloth coat flapping noisily around his legs. In an instant, he had disappeared into the darkness.

"Poor guy," Dara said. "Does anybody look after him?"

But Preston was still thinking. He hadn't been out west on 176 for months, but he could see it dipping and climbing its way toward the mountains, following the old wagon road along Lawson's Fork Creek, past the mills in Inman, through the orchards of tiny Gramling, the mountains looming larger until Hogback reared up over Landrum and then you hit the state line. Back in the fifties, before Vietnam and terror and nightmares, back when there was Mom and Dad and Eunice Babb at the junior high school prom, he had gone with his parents to the Blockhouse Steeplechase. There had been the old racecourse, just off 176, the one they used right up until the mid-eighties. "And there was that jump, right at the state line," he suddenly heard himself say.

Dara stared at him, then touched his arm lightly. "Maybe we should just stay in town tonight…"

"The Steeplechase. Don't you remember? There was the place where they jumped from North Carolina into South Carolina…and right there, right at the border, there's a stone marker."

* * *

There wasn't much traffic. Preston fidgeted with the radio, with Dara's CD collection, with the air conditioning, until Dara finally reached over from the driver's seat and slapped his hands. "Calm down, hon! What're you expecting to find out there, anyway? It's just an old hunka stone."

"It marks the place where the original Blockhouse used to be. They always had a little article about it in the race program and talked about it on WSPA when they carried the races on the radio. It started out as a fort, back before the Revolution. I bet even ol' Daniel must've spent some time there. Then it was a tavern, and who knows what all else. But it sat right on the state line, and when they finally tore it down, they put a marker there."

"Nice history lesson, professor, but you still haven't told me what we're looking for."

"I don't know. But if Chester knows, I want to know, too."

It was pitch dark when they finally turned off 176,

just a half mile or so before the border, and followed a narrow, winding road along the railroad bed down into a shallow valley. And there it was, no more than fifty feet back from the road, sitting in the pasture that had once been pounded by flying hooves and filled with the shouts of excited fans. Dara's flashlight played over the weathered surface of the slab, jutting up five feet from the moist earth. It looked almost prehistoric in the darkness, silent and watchful. Preston shivered.

They walked slowly around to the side of the stone facing away from the road. He didn't notice, at first, the dull white gleam at the base of the slab. But Dara did. "Oh my God, Preston!" She started to back away before Preston's steady grip on her arm calmed her.

He couldn't tell in the weak yellow light what sort of bone it was. Not enough of it projected out of the disturbed earth. But he could see one knobbed end, where a joint would have been; and he could see enough to recognize it as human. And there was something else. He bent down to retrieve a shiny, round piece of metal.

An owl hooted.

"Get your cell phone," he told Dara as calmly as he could. "Call Bo and tell him where we are and what we're looking at."

"But this can't have anything to with Phil Quake's murder. Out here?"

"Don't be so sure." He brought the flashlight close

to the delicate medal, long parted from the chain, and both from the wearer's neck; but even in the wavering beam, they could see what had been engraved on it. Just one word. A name, to be more precise. "Lynn," was all it said.

Chapter Nine

Bo Hunter braked hard as he pulled up to the pasture where Preston and Dara waited. Some young hotshot Preston had never seen before jumped out of the car with Bo. The stranger wore Ray-Bans pushed up above his handsome forehead and cradled in his nicely coifed blond hair. Preston wondered why he didn't just take the glasses off in the dark. Preston saw Dara smile at him as soon as the four met halfway between the stone and the cars. She took the stranger's hand a little too eagerly, Preston noted, as Bo introduced him as Jake, a SLED agent from Columbia.

"Hmmm," Bo said as he examined the "Lynn" medal, gripping it around the rim as Preston had, careful not to taint the evidence with his fingerprints.

"Tell you what, Jake," Bo suggested, "if you'll get

Dara to show you the rest of what they found, I'd like to talk to Preston here a minute."

Dara and Jake moved toward the stone and Preston followed Bo back toward the cars.

"We have a lead we could use some help on," Bo said to Preston when they were next to the road.

"I'm listening," said Preston.

"Well, we've been doing our homework at the radio station. The station manager has been really cooperative."

"You questioned all the employees?" Preston asked.

"Come on, Earley, give us a little credit. We've talked to everyone, searched Phil's personal belongings, and we've spent I don't know how many hours studying tapes and transcripts of his show."

"Yeah? So what turned up?"

"Nothing."

Preston frowned. "So what's this great lead you're talking about?"

"That's just it. When I say nothing. I mean a particular nothing."

Preston still frowned.

"A missing tape, Earley. From a show about ten months ago. There's no tape, no transcript, not even an agenda for the show that day. It's as if Phil's show didn't exist on that day. All the employees claim they have no idea what happened to the tape and nobody seems to remember what was on the show that day."

"Interesting," said Earley.

"It'll be a lot more interesting if we can find the tape."

"Is this where I come in?"

"You got it. As many Quake fans as there are around here, I know somebody has to have some old tapes. Can you get your hands on a tape of that show and be quiet about it?"

"I think I may know just the right source, Bo, but why'd you come to me? Why not let Jake the Snake over there earn his bucks?" Preston pointed to where Jake talked and gestured wildly with his hands while Dara stared admiringly.

"Jesus, Earley. You think I'd trust a green pretty boy with stuff that requires *trained* intuition? That kid can do all kinds of forensic and hi-tech hocus pocus, but when it comes to real detective work, he's clueless. Listen to this. On the way up here I got carried away talking about where I was when I got the news that JFK died and all that—I don't know how we got on the subject—but when I said to Jake that he wasn't even born yet when Kennedy was killed, he said, 'Oh, no, I was sitting right in my living room when CNN said the plane went down.' He thought I was talking about JFK *Junior* for Christ's sake. That's how clueless he is."

Jake's voice interrupted them.

"We need to get a crew out here to search and dig," he called from over at the stone.

"Whatcha got?" Bo called back as he and Preston

walked quickly toward Jake, Dara and the stone.

"Only part of an arm, but I bet we can find more." Jake spoke not so much to Preston and Bo as to his hand-held tape recorder. "Severed at the elbow," he continued into the little machine, "perhaps violently."

Preston wondered how an arm could be severed in any other way besides violently. "And it's been partially *burned*," Jake said.

Preston and Bo bent down to eye the bone on the ground more closely. Dara stood quietly.

Jake pocketed his tape recorder and drew his cell phone from his waist like some techie cowboy drawing his weapon at high noon. Preston grabbed Dara's phone from her as if it were a gun and a shootout were imminent. Suddenly, the investigation seemed to Preston to be a contest between him and this Adonis SLED man. Phone fight at the Blockhouse Corral. Preston dialed his buddy Lightman's number and said he was on his way to Gaffney.

Then he looked at Dara, remembered the lake and the boathouse.

"Geez, honey. I'm really sorry. But this is important."

To his surprise, she didn't seem upset.

"I know it's important, Preston. Go on to Gaffney and do what you have to do. Stay as long as you like."

Was there sarcasm in her voice?

"I'll be just fine." She looked at Jake as she said it, Jake who was speaking in a commanding voice to the gods of South Carolina law enforcement. Preston didn't like the glow on Dara's face, but he couldn't stay. He had a man to see about a tape.

* * *

Preston hadn't needed Daniel Morgan to tell him who could help him get the Quake tape the police needed. He hadn't seen his old Gaffney buddy Lightman in a long time, but he knew Lightman, whose real name was Rudy Jefferies, was the man he needed. Rudy was an electrician who'd earned the nickname "Lightman" by rigging light shows in nightclubs all over the Southeast. He loved to tinker with all sorts of lights and electronic gizmos. He was Phil Quake's cousin and biggest fan. He'd taped Quake's shows from the very beginning.

As Preston turned off Highway 29, just outside Gaffney, into Lightman's long winding driveway, his car activated a motion sensor which ignited rows of three flood lights on either side of the driveway. The instant daylight was so unsuspected that Preston was gripped by the feeling of going from utter darkness into some instant illumination, powerful enough to light the soul and terrify it at the same time, with just a simple turn of his steering wheel. Images of fires and sacrificial rites returned. Grotesques figures leaping about a stone.

He pressed the gas and was delivered to the next

surprise on Lightman's funhouse of a driveway, some softer, colored lights which eased his nerves a little bit so that he had the courage to ease cautiously up the driveway, startled only once more by a strobe light on a picnic table. He finally parked in the plain old sixty-watt glow of the front porch light.

When Preston rang the doorbell of Lightman's house, a piercing scream blared from a Bose speaker mounted over the door. Hundreds of white lights strung all around the porch chased each other for a few seconds, then faded.

The door gently opened.

"Greetings," Lightman said as he pushed open the screen and handed the tape out to Preston.

Preston looked at the tape, then at Lightman's scraggly bearded face.

"How did you know this is the tape I'm after, Rudy? I didn't tell you the date of the show on the phone."

"I figured it out," Lightman said, "cause some gooberlolly in a VW Bug was here ten minutes ago asking for this one. Said he was picking it up for you. I told him I didn't have it, then sent him on a wild goose chase, told him somebody out in McKown's Mountain tapes the show. I knew he was lying 'cause you would've told me if you were sending somebody else to pick it up."

Chapter Ten

BY MEG BARNHOUSE

Preston scratched the three-day growth of beard on his chin. He used to pull on his hair when he was confused, but there was so little of it left now, he had switched over to scratching his chin. How had the gooberlolly in the Bug found out about the tape? What did the goober—uh, person look like? Was the gooberlolly driving the lavender Bug where the shells were found or the rain-colored Bug that ran him off the road? Could a lavender Beetle look rain-colored under a darkling rain? Was his brain thinking in haiku now?

Preston became aware of a trickle of sweat dripping down his back. The cicadas were loud out here in the country in August. He couldn't understand what they were singing, though, so the meds were still working.

"Listen, can we take this inside? We're letting all

your cold air out."

Lightman stepped aside, and Preston came into the living room, heaving a sigh of relief as the chill of the air conditioning made breathing possible again. As he plopped down on the aging sofa, an agonized howl ripped the air. Preston sprang to his feet, icy adrenalin shooting through every nerve.

"Oh, man, that's Loretta." Lightman said, lowering himself into his recliner. "She sleeps under there. You squashed her. She'll get over it."

The cat flounced off into the kitchen and began noisily crunching on dry cat food in a bowl beside the refrigerator. Preston heard the back door slam, and the sound of quick footsteps. He stayed on his feet as the woman burst into the room.

"Sophie!" Preston gave Lightman's wife a squeeze and as much of a kiss as he thought he could get a way with.

"How are things down at the Universe-City, honeypot?" Lightman drawled.

"Don't even get me started!" Her mischievous smile was one of Preston's favorite things about Sophie. Along with her chocolate eyes, rounded body, gourmet cooking, dramatic flowing clothes, dark curly hair. And her encyclopedic knowledge of history. Yeah, her mind was his very favorite thing about her. That was his story and he was sticking to it.

"I heard you sit on Loretta. That yowl carries. What else did I miss?"

"We're talking about Phil's murder, baby." Lightman looked up at Preston. "I hope you and the gendarmes can figure out who done it. It's eating me up."

"Maybe this tape will give us something to go on."

"Do you think there might be something on it that got him killed?" Lightman asked. Sophie sat, listening, catching up.

"That's what I'm hoping we find out tonight."

"You want to listen to it here?" The couple looked at Preston eagerly.

"I don't see why not. After I get a description of the guy who showed up to collect it ahead of me." Preston sat back down, gingerly.

"Well, there was a strangeness about him."

"A—strangeness?"

"Yeah, I mean, it's like he was wearing jeans and a tie-dyed shirt. Beads. The whole hippie-retro Dead Head thing you'd expect to see climbing out of a purple VW Bug."

"Age?"

"Around nineteen, twenty, maybe."

"Height, weight, hair color?"

"Skinny. About Sophie's height, 5'8" or so."

"Black hair, super-pale skin, like a vegetarian, black fingernails."

"A mechanic, maybe? Grease under his nails?"

"No, man, that's what I'm trying to tell you. His fingernails were painted black. That's what was strange. More Marilyn Manson than Grateful Dead. Black hair, white skin. Goth. Totally. That's why it looked so ludicrous, him wearing tie-dye and driving the peace-and-love mobile."

"Goth?"

"Gothic—castles and death, black clothes, black hair. I lit for Ground Zero last weekend. Tons of Goth kids. Vomit opened for Sally's Death. Goth folks, they like vampires and blood, like that. Want to look like heroin addicts. Mostly nice suburban kids trying to suffer for Art."

"Art?" Preston was confused. "Is he some kid of cult leader for them?"

"No, *Art*, man," Lightman struck a pose with one limp hand over his heart and the other resting, palm out, on his forehead. The gesture looked incongruous from the hairy bear of a man in shorts and a Lynrd Skynrd T-shirt.

"Yeah, I've got one in my Mary Shelley class," Sophie chimed in. "She wears a three-inch-long metal fingernail on the little finger of her left hand. I would ask her what it's for, but I'm not sure I want to know."

Lightman heaved himself out of the recliner and headed into the kitchen, where he puttered around for a few minutes while Preston digested this new information and watched Sophie smooth the cat's fur with hypnotic strokes.

When he came back, he was carrying a tray with cold Coronas and slices of lime, a mound of cheese cut into squares and some Triscuits.

"What have you got so far that could help us foil the villains?" he asked, setting the tray on the coffee table.

"It might do you good to just lay out everything at once," Sophie said.

"Here is a piece of paper and a pen. Talk it out and write it down, and then you can go from there."

Preston couldn't see any reason not to tell them what he had. It might help, and it would keep his mind off of Dara and the SLED action figure back at the old Block House.

He told them about the three shots from the .38, the furniture from Dawkins Middle School that had been stored in the basement of the Palmetto Building ending up piled on Quake's body.

"I went to McCracken," said Lightman, apropos of nothing.

Preston listed the contents of Quake's pockets, including the thirteen gold dollars and the claim check for the .38. He described the letter from Lynn. He was about to tell them about finding Phil's heart neatly cut out and laid on his sleeve, but something inside his brain cleared its throat, and he left out that detail, telling them only that the body was sliced up some. He told them about getting run off the road by the Bug, the strange conversation with the beautiful young Lynn at the Regional Medical Center, and the medal with "Lynn" on it at the border stone where the Blockhouse used to be. He finished up with the human arm, not belonging to Phil Quake, he and Dara had found there.

"Like some kind of ritual human sacrifice," Preston said grimly. "I asked Theo and Leo about any cult of Dionysus around here, but they didn't take me seriously. I keep having these memories, like Druids or witches sacrificing somebody at a big bonfire by a standing stone."

"Witches are healers, not killers, and Druids probably never performed human sacrifice," Sophie snapped.

"Uh-oh, you're in for it now," Lightman said, grinning at his wife.

"The lurid information you were fed about Druids came from Julius Caesar's descriptions as his troops were at war with them. If you demonize a group of people, they are easier to kill. Are you sure you really saw that, Preston? In real life, I mean?" She looked at him intently. Preston knew she remembered some of his craziest times.

"Let's listen to the tape," Preston said, changing the subject.

The tape was puzzlingly benign. On it, Phil interviewed the woman who taught the weekend cooking school for the Southern Women's Home Show. "I was there!" Sophie cried. "It was last November sometime. She taught about fifty of us how to prepare Duck a L'Orange, from ingredient selection to handling the knives, to…" Her voice faded.

Lightman nodded. "Cooking school," he said sagely. "Chicks with sharp knives."

Chapter Eleven

Preston had lost a full day, but he was finally settled back into the Phil Quake case. The lost day was one of busted dreams, a quick trip to Lake Lure, and too many Spartan Stouts at R.J. Rockers. Soon after he left Gaffney and his meeting with Sophie and Lightman, lovely Dara had summoned him. When he arrived at the boathouse, she had cut him loose. As far as Preston knew she was off somewhere at that very moment mousing the hair of her young SLED agent.

"So is Jake the Snake gonna fix your fifty-five-year-old boathouse toilet when it clogs? Is SLED Sammy gonna ride around Chimney Rock at two in the morning looking for those overweight Weimaraners of yours rifling people's trash cans?"

Preston had crossed the line with the crack about

Reagan and Bush, her gray, cigar-shaped mega-pooches. "You're outta here, Earley!" Dara had screamed, throwing Preston's shaving kit, his shortie pajamas, and extra pair of underwear off the deck into the pine needles on the driveway.

"Pull yourself out of this tailspin of self-loathing, buddy boy," Preston mumbled to himself as he sucked down a B.C. Powder and pondered the name of the woman Sophie remembered as the one who had taught the cooking school on the particular weekend of Phil Quake's missing show.

"Peggy Sue Eerie," Sophie had repeated over and over. "And Preston, she also owns that cooking store in the Converse Plaza—Peggy Sue's Garlic Pot!" she added.

Back in detective mode, Preston drove out East Main to case the cooking shop. Preston didn't often come east of Daniel Morgan, but the detective knew Converse Plaza was the epicenter of east side chic, and Peggy Sue's Garlic Pot was where all Dara's friends learned how to julienne, truss, filet, and clarify their chicken stocks. As Preston fought a BMW and a Ford Excursion for a parking place, he was reminded of Dara's east side friends. He hoped he wouldn't run into any of them—Hunter, Logan or Madison. All those last names as first names. It gave him the heebie-jeebies.

A little bell tinkled when Preston opened the shop's door, and he was overwhelmed by the smell of garlic and the sound of a George Winston CD. The store was thickly provisioned with expensive pans, presses, processors, pot racks, and knives. Preston had never seen so many kitchen knives. There were hundreds of them in five or six display cases, some small as pocketknives, some large as Russian sabers.

In the back corner, elevated around the retail space and lighted like a prizefighting ring, was a large island with observation stools. In the center of the space was a silver gas range gleaming under the lights, ready for action. The stark light from the floods brought back the drums, the fire, the chants. He blinked the vision away.

Preston noticed a woman moving in the shadows cast by the large bar. She was busy with some pagan ritual. No, she was dusting among the pots and pans. She turned and smiled as Preston penetrated deeper into the shop.

"May I help you?" she asked.

Dara who? Preston thought. I have found my goddess. He was stunned by the clerk's thick, black curls and ancient beauty. Then Preston's eyes were drawn downward for a moment to the woman's dangling right sleeve. Missing arm! the detective in him reported to his internal notebook.

"Are you…Peggy Sue?" he finally said, recovering his balance.

"No, Peggy Sue's at D'Bordieu," the woman smiled.

"At Debby Doo?"
"Yes, at D'Bordieu with Frank. For the week."

* * *

"He broke," Bo said when Preston returned his police buddy's page that afternoon.
"Who broke, Bo?"
"Our number one suspect," Bo said. "Chester."
"Chester?"
"Doughnuts," Bo explained.
"Doughnuts?"
"I know it sounds like an unconventional law enforcement technique, but when we picked him up we put him in solitary and withheld the doughnuts. After 24 hours he finally gave us what we wanted."
"A confession?"
"Not exactly a confession, though I think we're close to charging him."
"Charging Chester?"
"Murder one. Two counts. He's the only one who has known about both murders."
"Both murders?"
"You know, Phil Quake and the arm."
"What did Chester tell you?"
"Why don't you just meet me down on Magnolia Street in an hour. I think you'd like to see what we're doing."
"Come on, Bo. Just give me a hint."

"Okay, Earley. You know that house Frank Eerie moved last October?"

"Frank Eerie? The developer?" Preston exclaimed.

"Well, Chester says there's an important clue under that house Eerie moved to make way for that new hotel."

"A cover-up?"

"So to speak."

"How's Chester?"

"He's a little loopy from all the sugar, but he's going down and show us where to dig."

"Dig?"

"Preston, I think the rest of body number two is buried under that house."

"Don't bet on it," Preston said dryly.

"You should have heard Chester singing like a canary when we opened that last box of Krispy Kremes."

"Let me get this straight, Bo. You think Chester, a homeless man with a weakness for doughnuts, is in cahoots with the most powerful developer in Spartanburg to cover up a murder by moving a Victorian house three blocks?"

"Well, we haven't got it all figured yet, but when we get that house moved…"

* * *

The Dupre house was a huge, gray birthday cake,

all turrets and layers. Preston noted how its location, next to the Magnolia Street Cemetery, added to the mystery, especially if Bo's hunch was right and there was forensic work to be done.

Preston slipped past the yellow crime scene tape the city's finest had strung all across the front of the lot. He saw Bo leaning against a patrol cruiser, sharing a final half-dozen Krispy Kremes with Chester.

"This is one mess you're in, Chester," Preston said, patting his friend on the shoulder.

"Chester's happy to help out the authorities," he said, licking the sugar off his fingers. "More help, more doughnuts."

"Where's your SLED sidekick?" Preston asked.

"He's due any minute," Bo said. "He had some business up at Lake Lure."

The tractors from the moving company groaned against the long beams under the house, and for a half-hour the structure crept toward the empty lot next to it.

"More! More!" Chester kept screaming. "It's further under. Right in the middle! That where the pirates buried the treasure!"

"How did you get Eerie's permission?" Preston asked.

"He's out of town, so we took out a search warrant," Bo said.

"Well, Bo, look at that," Preston said, pointing out to the street. "There's that VW Bug again."

The lavender Beetle puttered up Magnolia, slow as a funeral.

"Well, I'll be damned," Preston said. "We got enough probable cause to pick up the driver?"

"Naw, we'll let him go for now. We've got bigger fish to fry," Bo said

The house lurched one final time and came to a stop on the next lot. Bo walked Chester into the middle of the space where the house had rested for almost a year. "Okay, Chester, show us the gold."

"Here," Chester said, jumping up and down on a mound of red clay.

"Here, here, here." He said, moving to three other spots, forming a square in the bare space where the house had been.

"Four spots?" Bo asked. "Looks like a pattern."

"Two times two," Chester said.

The officers dug in each spot Chester pointed out. At each spot, a foot deep in the ground, they found a piece of plywood. When they pulled the plywood up, they found a little square chamber made from old bricks.

"What is it?" Bo said to Preston as they squatted down looking into the first hole.

"A Sugar-n-Spice to-go box," Preston laughed.

"Don't touch it. Could be a bomb!" Jake the Snake screamed, approaching from the rear.

"Could be an eight-month-old hash-a-plenty, too," Preston said, glancing up at his rival.

Chapter Twelve

Preston Earley was as down as a stockbroker in a bear market. His low bowled lower than Chester coming down off Krispy Kreme's. After hours of soaking up coffee with Bo and Jake the Snake SLED agent, the country songs on the jukebox at the Waffle House were making more sense than this case.

Preston tried walking as a way to clear his head. He wanted to drop thirty-five cents in the nearest pay phone and beg Dara to at least talk to him. Her voice on the phone gave him more juice than most women's whole bodies. But after her flame-thrower rejection, he felt it might be hazardous to his hearing to even try a phone call.

What was Chester's connection? Who stole the tape of the cooking show? Could the old lady at the flower shop really hate Quake enough to kill him?

The perp was definitely sicker than Stephen King. Cutting the hands off the second victim and putting them in one of the Sugar-n-Spice boxes not only strained good manners, it would definitely lead to an ID. Preston was equally confused by the contents of the second box, dozens of cassette tapes, most of them broadcasts of radio shows—Phil Quake, Pal Crystal, Bone Crusher Battle—all the local talk-show guys, plus the audios from TV newscasts, play-by-play from footballs games, weather reports, hog futures, all male voices, some of them even from other parts of the country.

And photographs, cut to pieces in the third box, young women, older men, formula crap from too many Hollywood romances, and of course, that fourth box, maybe strangest of all. Empty.

Who goes to the trouble of ditching an empty box under plywood just before a monster house gets moved to cover the evidence?

Preston walked Hearon Circle letting headlights ballet around his head. He listened to the roar and hum of traffic and the conveyors inside Flowers Bakery and thought the inside of his brain was much, much busier.

How did Chester keep coming up with clues? Why was he reluctant to help? Why in the Sam Hill didn't he just ask him?

He mounted his truck in the parking lot of the Waffle House and looked at Bo and Jake still drawing diagrams on napkins inside.

The quick drive down Asheville Highway gave him time to think. He didn't want time to think. You're going to question Chester after Bo's had his claws into him? You think you can get more out of ol' Ches than that tinhorn sheriff? Where did that come from? Maintain, Preston. Look at your watch. 10:27. Spartanburg, S.C. Football season. You do the crossword in the HJ. Calm, drive the truck. Ten frigging 27. And a one and a two and a three and 10:28. Grounded.

He walked Morgan Square and down Magnolia Street. He saw Chester before Chester saw him. The homeless loon almost jumped out of his skin when Preston called his name.

"Ooh, you scared me, Muffin Man. Got a dollar?"

"A lot more than that if you'll solve this crime."

"Bo's almost done. Give him time."

"Bo dudn't know if the sun's gonna rise in the morning. What makes you think he can solve this one?"

"What did they bury under that house?" Chester asked.

"Who's they?"

"Who's they? Who's they?" Chester started to echo, but Preston clapped his hands together in a loud pop and spat through his teeth.

"Don't start with me, Ches, or I'll never buy you another muffin for a thousand years." He heard himself and wondered which of them might be crazier.

"What you want, Preston? It past my bedtime," Chester tried to stutter.

"You know what I want, you crazy sack of Siberian snake crap. Who's doing this? Who killed Phil Quake? Whose hands are in that box? Who in the name of Holy Hannah is doing this?"

"I can't tell, Pres. You know I can't tell. Nobody wanna know. Bo don't wanna know. I can't tell, Pres. Lemme go to bed, Pres. Bye, Pres. You kiss Dara for me," Ches babbled and ran. Preston felt like he'd gotten all he could get.

He let him run, ambled to his apartment, and lay on his back tracing the street light on his ceiling while the caffeine found a home in his blood, in his brain. Just before sleep, he looked down at his hands.

The radio station was losing patience. He'd lost Dara. He kept listing the suspects—jilted poet, frustrated cooking queen, women, and dear, dear Lynn. Who could forget Lynn? Who was he trying to kid? He'd thought of nothing else. Sure questioning Chester had seemed like a good idea at the time, but more dead ends? Had there been anything there? Did Chester let anything slip? Chester knew too much not to know it all, but he was obviously too scared to talk, and maybe too crazy to make a decent witness.

But lovely, lovely auburn-haired, coed, the girl in the picture, Lynn. There was another story. Had she ever been a guest on the Phil Quake show? Was she his guest off the air, his trip down memory lane, his dream come true? Oh, surely not. Good grief. Phil Quake?

But who was she?

Who was this Irish beauty who stalked his dreams? Had Dara been reading his dreams? Did she know how often they danced in Morgan's shadow, how many times the tips of his fingers had brushed her neck in dreamland? Had Dara overheard his fantasy of Lynn whispering, "Preston," when he should only have been thinking of his one true love?

True love, hell. He was on the street, and maybe the street was where he might find Lynn.

He remembered the general telling him it was right in front of his face.

He drove to Converse College and strolled into the library, asked for the most current copy of the yearbook. This had taken him this long? What was he thinking? How could he have missed this detail?

It didn't take long. There she was. Page 63. Four rows down, three rows over. Lynn?

No. Not that last name.

Had to be a coincidence. Couldn't be. Nothing to it.

He punched the numbers on the pay phone in the library. When the voice came on the other end, he asked, "You got a niece or a cousin or something at Converse?"

"How about my daughter?" the other party asked.

"I didn't know you had kids," Preston said flatly.

"Divorced a long time ago. I was pretty blown away when she came to Converse. I still don't see much of her. You know how college kids are."

"Yeah, I know how college kids are. Listen, I hate to ask you to do this, but could you meet me at the police station in about an hour?"

"Why?"

"Your daughter's picture was found the night Phil Quake was killed."

Chapter Thirteen

Jake looked up from the photo on the conference room table and grinned. "She's a babe, a looker, the kinda woman a man like you calls a real dame."

Preston looked at Jake as if he were a particularly nasty specimen under the microscope in a forensics lab. "Snake, you've been reading way too many cheap detective novels. But then—maybe that's the way they train you SLED boys these days."

Jake's eyes took on a hard look. "What's the matter, Preston? Lost your sense of humor, too?"

Preston couldn't help but laugh. "Snake, you just keep feeling good about yourself. Make jokes as long as you can. But if I were you, I'd start checkin' over my VISA bills and keepin' an eye on my bank account balance. 'Cause the only thing you've found is a quick route to the poor house."

Jake stood up and started around the table toward Preston. Bo quickly held up one grease-stained hand and stopped Jake. "Will you two give it a rest?"

Jake and Preston glared at one another, but Jake sat back down. "Now that's more like it...we're on the same team fellas. We gotta work together on this, or we're never gonna solve these crimes."

"What do you mean, crimes? We've got one murder. You think there's been more?" asked Jake.

"If you're not careful, I'm gonna develop the same low opinion of you that Preston has." Bo paused and took another bite of fried chicken. "Hey, you fellas want some o' this?"

Jake shook his head. Preston reached over and took a yeast roll. "No one makes yeast rolls like Wade's."

"You got that right, old buddy. Now listen up, Jake. We've got Phil Quake dead and mutilated—heart cut out of his body and sewn to his sleeve with pink yarn. We've got one human arm found at the Blockhouse and we've got two severed hands in a Sugar-n-Spice to-go box. You know, some souvlaki would be really good right now. On top of that we've got an attempt at murder by whoever tried to run Preston off the road. Add to that, the little episode with Lightman, and someone knowing we were going after a tape only he would have, and we have got some more mess to try and figure out. Murder, attempted murder, lies, cover-ups and conspiracies. Son, we've got a lot more than a single murder happenin' here. We've got the makins' of a major motion picture."

Preston rolled his eyes and grinned at his old friend. "Who do you think they'll get to play you, Bo?"

"Well, Mel Gibson makes a pretty believable cop."

Preston just shook his head. "Finish your meal. I see you only got the family-of-four takeout size, and I know you'll want to be finished with that pint of creamed corn by the time Baxter gets here."

"The green beans weren't bad either."

Jake looked back and forth between Bo and Preston. "Spartanburg's finest," he said.

"You got that right," said Bo. "Now, Preston, tell me how Baxter Eerie fits into this."

"He's her father," and Preston pointed to the photograph on the table.

There was dead silence. Baxter Eerie was the first cousin of developer, Frank Eerie. A new twist had been added. The mysterious Lynn was an *Eerie.*

"How did you find out?" asked Bo.

"I suppose I could have just called the hospital and asked her name since she was there doing a project when I was in the ER, but I wanted to be thorough. I went to the Converse library and looked through annuals. She's still a student. In fact, she's just nineteen. I called Baxter and told him to meet us here."

"I didn't know Baxter had any kids," said Bo.

"Neither did I. Apparently it was a brief marriage

to someone he met at a Marshall Tucker concert in 1980. The marriage didn't last, but our friend Lynn was the result. Baxter told me over the phone that she grew up in Tampa with her mother, and they've always had a close father-daughter relationship. He said he wants to make sure his little girl is not in any trouble."

"Well, I sure didn't see this coming. Phil Quake was having an affair with a nineteen-year-old Converse girl. And not just any Converse girl, but a member of one of Spartanburg's oldest and wealthiest families. Way to go, Phil. Whoa!"

"Not so quick, Bo. Lynn told me in the hospital that she had been interviewed on Phil's show about a project she was doing on people's responses to trauma. The note and the picture seem to hint at something more, but we've got no proof. That's why I asked Baxter to meet me here and…"

"And what?" asked Jake.

"And to bring his daughter," said Preston.

"Dadgummit, Preston. You haven't even given me any prep time."

"I know, Bo. Frankly you do better when you haven't been spending a lot of time trying to figure out all the nuances of an interrogation. Don't forget about almost causing Chester to O.D. on doughnuts."

"Gimme a break. Chester may not be the murderer, but he sure led us to those boxes."

"True, but I think Lynn and her daddy are going to get us a lot closer to the killer, or killers, than Chester."

"Maybe," spoke up Jake. "Then again, maybe she's the one guilty of murder."

Suddenly there was a knock at the door, and a police sergeant walked into the room. "Lieutenant, you were waiting on Baxter Eerie?"

"Yeah."

"We just got an emergency call from security at Converse College. It's Eerie, Baxter Eerie. They found him in his car beside Belk dorm. He's dead."

* * *

The ride to Converse was quick and made in stunned silence. Preston's mind was racing with too many thoughts to articulate. Just as it had seemed they were going to start getting to the bottom of the whole mess, this had to happen. Not only that, Baxter was a friend. Now Preston was angry.

They were met at the entrance to the parking lot by a uniformed officer already on the scene. "He's over here."

Crossing over the yellow tape marking off the crime scene, and moving past emergency personnel, they looked into Baxter Eerie's silver Mercedes. Baxter was slumped over the wheel with a large kitchen knife protruding from between his shoulder blades. In the floorboard of the car were thirteen gold one-dollar coins.

The officer spoke up. "There's a girl wants to talk to you, Earley. Says you're probably expecting her. Her name's Lynn. She's in the lobby of Belk with two guys from Wofford. A Fletcher Samson and David Boyle. She said to tell you they're just friends she called to wait with her until you got here."

Jake and Bo exchanged glances and followed Preston into the lobby. A beautiful young redhead s at sobbing on the couch between two young men. She looked up when they entered the room.

"Thank God," she sobbed. Running up to Preston, she threw her arms around him and buried her head in his shoulder.

Chapter Fourteen

BY SUSAN BECKHAM JACKSON

Preston went early to Baxter Eerie's funeral. He thought sitting in the quiet serenity of the sanctuary at the Episcopal Church would calm him. Under the dark wooden arches with the glorious images in stained glass all around him, it would be a place he could think more clearly. A place where murder, chaos, and severed bodies seemed far away. And the mixed-up voices in his head could sort themselves and gain perspective.

On top of all the existing madness in Spartanburg, the media had gone crazy after Baxter's death. Reporters coming from everywhere, and stories running national across the AP wires. Things were getting out of control. Every time he turned a corner, it seemed someone was coming at him, wanting gory details. It was big all right, like the general said, and getting bigger all the time.

He thought of Baxter's beautiful black-eyed daughter enduring the publicity, too, in the midst of her father's death. He made up his mind then; she couldn't be the perpetrator. Not just because she was beautiful and he adored her or even that he felt sorry for her. He was thinking much more clearly than that. It just wasn't logical, that was all. Lynn couldn't have killed Quake because she wouldn't have been so daft as to leave her picture near his corpse. And that was that. Or was it?

He was really humming now. Maybe he should come to church more often. Could she be a step ahead of him? Outwitting him with some weird kind of reverse psychology? Psychology must be her thing, trauma victims and maybe more. Might she have purposely planted her picture on Quake to lure the investigation away from her? Like some kind of decoy to misdirect the trail?

He saw her lovely face again, as he saw it upon waking after two days of blackout in the hospital. He had recognized that vision immediately, even if he hadn't been able to name how. And later he'd thought it was from the picture. But now he wasn't so sure. It was like he recognized all of her, not just the face.

The organ music started, slow and somber. His thoughts moved to white rocks and seats in a circle. Of one gigantic fire and wild figures dancing all around. He knew now how Young Goodman Brown felt. That literature-made-famous Puritan he'd studied in school at Wofford. Goodman Brown had seen fire shoot forth on a rock and form a glowing arch while fiendish worshippers beckoned him. And Goodman Brown hadn't known either whether he had fallen asleep and only dreamed a wild dream or whether it was real.

Preston stared at the church altar cloaked in funeral flowers, the casket veiled in blood-red roses. The sight held him quiet, spellbound; his mind at this moment was as clear as it could ever get. He definitely had to come to church more often. Something new, that had seemed insignificant until now, played through his head.

Paramedics hadn't taken him to the hospital. No one knew who had. It had been late at night with nearly no one around. The hospital staff found him propped in an emergency room chair. They assumed a good Samaritan, quick on the scene of the accident, but not wanting to get involved, had delivered him and left. He shivered realizing this thing he had tried to make a dream was real. All the dark dancing figures. What had they done to him? Was their purpose just to scare him away?

People were beginning to fill in the pews. Preston moved to the end of his row to make room. More people and more people kept coming. Lots of people he'd never seen. Baxter was a good guy, had friends, was a member of the long established and reputable Eerie family. But all this? Preston thought, watching the ushers bring in folding chairs.

After the service, the mob stayed respectful in the building. He stood in the aisle behind a knot of young women, their heads together whispering. College friends of Lynn's, probably. But once on the front lawn, everyone pushed and shoved, all to get a view of the family. Most of the strangers, it appeared, had come to gawk, enticed by the infamy of the case no doubt, wanting a look at something, but at what they didn't know. Even the television cameras were rolling. Preston wedged through to the sidelines at the edge of the church cemetery.

He hoisted himself onto a raised marble slab above an Eerie grave where he could get a better view. Eeries were planted all around this spot, their headstones like a mushroom garden. It'd been years since a person was buried in the churchyard. He looked at the new hole dug in a coveted remaining plot. No spaces remaining except to old families like Eeries. He rubbed his bashed shoulder with one hand and reached to unlace the shoe of his stomped foot with the other. Human beings. No wonder he talked to statues.

Bent down over his shoe, he almost missed it. But he looked up just in time to see the old woman huddle her arms around Lynn Eerie and usher her away from the people trying to talk to her. Preston couldn't help but gape himself at Miss Lucille as she pulled her thick-ankled leg into the funeral car behind Lynn and closed the door. The car wasn't going anywhere at the moment, but it offered shelter. And then, he saw Chester, like he'd walked up from nowhere, knocking on their car window. They ignored his gesture.

"What in God's name," Preston said loudly enough from his perch to catch the attention of the assistant rector not so far away. The rector turned toward him, folded his arms across his white robe, questioning. "Oh, so sorry. Nothing intended," Preston said, bowing toward the rector and tipping gingerly off the stone. Best for him to go home. Straight home. And make a list of people to watch and to question. Tops on the list would be Chester early in the morning. Enough was enough. Whatever bribe they'd given him to keep silent could surely be overcome. He'd go out first thing in the morning. Chester was always up way before dawn puttering around the city, finding chores to do.

* * *

The day dawned with pink and purple streaks sweeping over an even pale blue pallet. A beautiful Indian summer's day, Preston thought, and not many more like this before the chill of fall set in. Yes, even without Dara's arms to look forward to, Preston felt poetic again. And he had energy to spare, even with staying up half the night plotting his plan. He was ready to crack this case.

He walked down the street in front of his apartment and gazed toward Morgan Square. He looked up toward the face of General Morgan just starting to gleam in the day's new light. Then he looked down at a dark mass in Morgan's shadow. He rushed forward, already knowing before he arrived. It was Chester, his friend, lying there. Preston bent toward his body, saw the chest had been cut open and retched. Chester's heart was gone.

Instinctively, he searched. Nothing on Chester's sleeve or anywhere nearby on the ground. Then he looked up and saw on other side of the statue where the sword sliced out into air. Chester's heart hanging like an ornament on the tip of the blade.

"Oh, God, oh, no." Preston's voice howled across the square. He choked, kept choking and couldn't stop. Creating commotion. People would hear and come. He had to cover Chester. Preston managed to remove his thin jacket and cover the upper body. Then he stood and shook, the breathless choking subdued to jerking pains in his chest. He hadn't thought once about Chester in danger of savage Dionysus worshippers, frenzied poets, or both or otherwise. If anything, he'd assumed being dimwitted kept Chester safe. But it was rationalization. He'd only been following his own agenda. When he'd known all along Chester knew too much.

Chapter Fifteen

Just as the backdoor of the forensics van slammed and the body bag zipped for the M.E.'s wagon, Jake the Snake and his SLED cowboys wheeled up to slow things down. But by then Preston was a refugee from the scene, watching it all almost safely through his window from above.

The zipper retraced its track for Jake to prod and poke, as if that would do any good, running his mouth all the while into his tape recorder amid the circle of nodding lackeys from Columbia.

Retreating from the window, Preston sat heavily down and opened his hand to stare at an oblong rock, smooth as if creek rounded, flecked with tiny mica that gave him little enough light now. It fit easily in his palm, nearly disappeared when he closed his hand on it, just as it had been hidden in Chester's fist.

Preston had found it only because he wanted to look at anything besides the yellow grimace, the gaping hole where something by all rights should have been beating, and his eyes had fallen on the man's right fist, filthy with grime from the scratched nails back to the barked knuckles. Gently he peeled the thick fingers open, expecting a last crumpled muffin, when this cylinder of stone had rolled to the paving. Feeble defense against a knife; even the short fall from Chester's palm to the pavement had chipped it. A stone with a fault at every angle.

Whoa.

He found himself on his feet again, still staring at his hand. All this right in front of the flower shop and Lucille Stone too. Could Chester have meant that, a last form of witness before life turned its back on him?

He recalled a day now months old, maybe longer, when coming out from The Sandwich Factory he'd happened upon Lucille giving Chester such a tongue lashing for idle loitering on her sidewalk that afterward Chester had slowly brought forth the closest thing to an unkindness Preston had ever heard from his lips: "Man, that woman put the ugh in ugly."

He pursued his lips to ponder Bo Hunter's need to learn of that incident right now and wandered back to the window to look down on the scene again: the too-familiar tape strung like a sickly decoration around the base of Morgan's pedestal, everybody gone now but a bored cop scratching his belly and hoping for lunch. And yeah, he'd have to explain to Bo later about tampering again with crime scene evidence, but figured he practically had a license by now.

Preston lifted the stone between index and thumb, examined its length in silhouette. Not perfectly round, of course. Flatter than he'd thought, a little jagged on one end, his fingertip told him. And while he stared another shape fell across his mind's eye, the shadow of the border stone cast by headlights and held up by memory now to match the slight shade of this small replica. Then the dream from the hospital woke in his brain again, black figures in antic poses, limbs all agog at acute angles, masked eyes reddened by a leaping bonfire.

His mind began to rifle its gray contents for the classics taught him in his misspent youth, so misspent that all he could recover now was Theo and Leo's old joke about Greek literature, divine retribution, and ripping somebody else's pants: Euripides, Eumenides. (You-rip-a-dees...You-mend-a-dees). He fell to the gap-toothed set of brown and mildewed Funk & Wagnall's that he tried assembling on grocery store trips fifteen years or so ago, figuring a private eye might need an intellectually respectable backdrop for visiting clientele, and at three bucks a volume it sure beat hell out of the Britannica. Please, God, he had the right volumes, or some of them anyway, and began to follow the alphabetic trail. Eumenides, when he puzzled beyond his misspellings, led him to the

Furies, Euripides to the Bacchae, but he'd never bought volume two somehow, so he turned to Dionysus instead.

Wild rites, wild rites was what he shook loose from the words, wine and steamed bodies and transcendence of identity round a holy fire. Spirits of punishment avenging wrongs within families, harrowing violators of hospitality. Mister Funk and Mister Wagnall repaid his investment this day—if Preston were right. At any rate, he looked at the calendar marking the moon's fullness tomorrow night and, scratching in another three days' growth of quickly graying beard, knew where he'd be when it rose.

* * *

This was all about crossing borders, Preston thought. The boundaries were all called off here.

There before him was the spitting image of his dream. He had thought it only delusion, another hallucination to live with, like the others. But there they were.

Crouched in the high weeds of a rise, he'd watched them assemble, prepare. Standing at a distance from the border stone was a fluted column, broken off and probably from Final Reduction, with a Lone Ranger mask taped to it and a girdle of fake ivy belting on a burgundy swag, probably also from Final Reduction. In the space between stone and column, they dumped armloads of brambles and branches, stuffed in for tinder crumpled to-go boxes from Sugar-n-Spice.

But who they were remained shrouded behind the masks, blank and white, and beneath flowing hooded robes, some fawn, some black.

All this they accomplished by torchlight, held high by a circle of votaries that the workers joined when their tasks were done. Then there was perfect silence. No shout, no song, no orgy. Preston stared out beneath a furrowed brow, vaguely disappointed. This wasn't what Messrs. Funk and Wagnall had promised at all. Then a stick broke. Behind him.

"Get up, son."

Nobody'd called him *son* in twenty years and he didn't take kindly to its introduction now. Just as he reared up they set upon him, five, six, hell, a baker's dozen for all he knew, his arms crooked behind him, head jerked back by his thinning hair, a tight line round his throat.

By the time he was bound shirtless to the border stone the fire five paces away was lit and the worshippers, if that's what you called them, were revolving in an orbit that took in him, the fire, and the column beyond. A big one in fawn he'd not seen until now approached with a large wooden salad bowl and dumped something darkly scarlet on his head. It ran like molasses and clotted in his eyes. He tried to bar his lips, but they pulled his hair again and forced his jaws open so that the liquid oozed past his teeth.

He tried spitting, but they tightened the noose, then he got the cloying sweetness on his tongue and almost instantly felt his muscles smooth out.

The big one backed away, and beneath the half mask Preston saw a smile too precise to be masculine. A priestess then, or something. He found himself returning the smile, pleased with the validity of his research so far.

Behind her, tongues of flame sawed the August wind. The circle was spinning fast now, in a dance that threw up on the trees in the near distance a shadow world of mimic dancers arching over them all. Go tell the Spartans this, Preston thought, his head lolling on the stone, his eyes to the sky.

Like some nature documentary in fast forward, the full moon went through all its phases and back while he blinked. Clouds sprinted from horizon to horizon, vines grew from moss to treetop and twined like snakes with others from neighboring trees until the forest was one net between him and the stars blacked out beyond. Beautiful faces whirled and brayed aloud their laughter. A stag leapt a fallen oak at the limit of the light, pursued by a wolf with opalescent eyes. A bull bellowed far off. The priestess, or whatever, shimmied so that her hood fell away, loosing oiled ringlets that gleamed and writhed all black in the firelight. Then the leaves all reddened and fell and were covered with snow and his teeth chattered an instant till the cool spring rain drenched him with a hot summer wind and the late August night came back before the dancers had completed one circle about their pyre, torches thrust aloft by slender alabaster hands, but from the other wide sleeves no hands came. Preston, man, he thought, you been roped and tied by a bunch of one-armed girls. He laughed but couldn't hear it.

The priestess approached, dancing with a new precise smile. His dizziness left him only when he saw the blade. A butcher knife as long as the forearm that held it above him.

Two hands with black fingernails suddenly gripped the forearm, a voice from a black cloak cried out, "Peggy Sue!"

The priestess turned, the blade shot firelight in Preston's clotted eyes.

"Dennis, you idiot," she hissed. "You know this is all part of what is fated to be."

The figure in black froze a moment, then released her, folding its black-nailed hands as the priestess turned her mask again to Preston.

He tried to shout "Murderer!" into that face, must have somehow succeeded, for she paused.

"No, no, it's not about death at all, Mr. Earley. Not at all. It's about rebirth."

The blade sang in the air and Preston closed his eyes to its flash.

Chapter Sixteen

Terror will eat you up. But then let that moment go on and on and on and terror seems to lose its way—like it's got no idea where to go or what it's supposed to do.

That happened. Something got in the way—hot darn!—between his chest and the butcher knife. But he couldn't bring himself to open his eyes. That woman was wild—prehistoric. Open his eyes and she'd remember what she was doing. One chance he had—and that was playing possum.

It dawned on him he couldn't hear one thing. Had he gone deaf? Was it that danged molasses-poison setting to work? Was this hyena of a woman waiting for that molasses-poison to kick in before she carved him up?

A crackle from the fire. Insect screech. Thank the

spooky powers that be—at least his ears were working. Only—there wasn't one solitary human sound as far as he could make out. Had he gone out of his mind? Was he having a blasted nightmare?

At that his eyes popped open. Looked out on pitch dark—except for lurid flickers from the devil's fire. Light enough to grasp that woman was in front of him—all those other creepy figures still as stone. Like they were waiting for something.

He couldn't make her eyes out in the dark—the red was glowing out from behind the medusa head. But bless those heavens—she had dropped her arm.

His eyes got locked to where he guessed her eyes would have to be. His own were still getting used to this danged dark.

Now he was catching on to some glitter that had to be her eyes. Glued on his the way his eyes had got themselves glued on hers. Dadgummit—his breathing was changing. He could feel it slowing down. Something bad was getting hold of him. He's got to fight this thing. He made a stab at looking away from this devil but his head wouldn't scarcely move. Jiminy Cricket—he couldn't unglue his eyes.

A sound out of her—a low and calm-like sound like he hadn't heard out of her.

"Don't be afraid of me," she said. "You aren't afraid, are you?"

"Heck no, I ain't afraid." That's what he said, but he sure as heck didn't have a mind to say that thing.

Those words had jumped out of his mouth not caring a fig what he thought.

So this blasted woman was hypnotizing him! Okay, he was highly susceptible to such tricks—that general clung to him like an incubus. But this fiend wouldn't get her claws in him. He was a man—he had a will of his own.

She was saying, "Preston Earley, you are safe. We intend to set you free. You will not be harmed, because we do not harm. You don't believe that—you haven't bothered to use your head. You've joined those idiots who've brainwashed you—people who think if people have secrets they've got evil secrets. But suspicions don't surprise us any longer. Nothing surprises us any longer—even outlandish murders. Can't you see, you numbskull? Those kinky murders are designed—those sick fiendish murders are meant to point at us, turn the whole Hub City to blaming us. But this lunatic city's been taken in. You've been taken in, Mister Earley. We are not murderers. We do quite the opposite of murder. You don't understand that yet but you will understand. Is your mind open to me?'"

"Yes, ma'am, my mind is sure wide open to you." He didn't seem to have any choice in what he said to this woman. Yet—Holy moly—this time he took himself seriously. When it made no sense to believe this butcher-knife woman. When here he was, lying here quite peacefully tied up, and believing every lying word coming out of this butcher-knife woman's mouth. But, Jiminy Cricket, he had a few things to get straight—and he couldn't somehow manage to get his questions out.

"The knife," she said. "The ropes. That's what you're aiming to ask. Well, it's surely got to be obvious we're a secret society and you've invaded us, so it's our turn to put a little fear in you. Still, a threat is a long way from a deed. But here you are, and you've got to learn a few things. Yes, indeed, we have our rituals, knives. And no, we don't dismember. We don't kill. We merely bind one arm beneath our robes. That's one way we rehearse our interconnection, our interdependence with the universe. We aim to work in perfect cooperation. So you see—by binding one part of ourselves, we sacrifice physical strength. We're after quite another form of strength. We're after the kind of strength that matters. If humankind is meant to survive, then every human being must learn to depend on only the strength that matters. We haven't done that in this country. We don't have any inkling about the strength that matters. For one thing, America's forgotten sacrifice. This city's forgotten sacrifice—when it ought be obvious that every gain demands its sacrifice."

His eyes hadn't flickered away one jot. But he noted her nod to the hooded figures beside her. He was conscious, while she was giving her spiel, of figures approaching him. And out of the corner of his eye he caught an odd hand movement—some gesture of complicity—with him. His breathing quickened—heavens to Betsy—it was Lynn! Now Lynn was behind his back, working with some other creature. Her fingers were on his back! The heat rose to his cheeks. She and that other body were busy untying knots—he could feel the way they were moving—with only one hand each. These peculiar women were working this rope in the dark, cooperating in silence, until the rope fell down his arms and into his lap. Again her warm hand rested on his back. Again her hand slid over his skin as she was getting up.

He was free. But still, he didn't move. Still the woman held his eyes while he was conscious of Lynn, while he was dimly conscious of the hooded figures slowly beginning to move around in a circle.

"Now," she said, "you may see one piece of our ritual of knives. You'll see we're dedicated. You'll see we practice concentration. You'll see we practice trust and absolute cooperation. But understand—this kind of trust is power, and men are afraid of women having power. It's true—to learn this trust we have to bind ourselves together, we have to practice radical cooperation, we have to do the things most difficult of all things not impossible. And the very idea has turned some men barbarian—you'll have to ask yourself what makes them terrified. And tell me if you learn—somebody's got to learn. Because they'll dismember even Chester to get us framed—don't you see? We're slipping out of control—they think. They're drumming up the craving for witch trials. Do you begin to understand?"

"I begin to understand."

"But do you FEEL you understand? If you FEEL the truth of what I'm saying it will burn through your veins and you'll get to the bottom of things. Or else this town is doomed."

"I feel what you are saying."

She stared, and then she smiled and dropped to her knees and took his hand. "Watch quietly then," she said, "and understand."

Chapter Seventeen

BY DENO TRAKAS

The ritual began. The hooded, robed and masked figures formed a tight circle around the fire between the border stone, where Preston watched with the priestess, and the fluted white column. With fuzzy math, he counted thirteen of them. In his drugged or poisoned condition, he looped in and out of focus, and on one of the loops, he imagined the scene from above, and it looked like some letter of the Greek alphabet that he remembered vaguely from his fraternity days. Yeah, that's what this was like, some weird fraternity or sorority thing. Yet something familiar.

Then that dadgum priestess—what was her name?—let go of his hand, slid the butcher knife from the belt in her robe and raised it like a dagger, then jammed its blade into the ground between his outstretched legs. At that signal, all the one-armed figures bent over and stabbed their knives into the ground likewise. A fat white snake appeared, wrapped around the arm of one of the women, but then it turned into a coil of rope. She held it out to the woman next to her—according to the priestess, they were all women, except for what's-his-name who had roughed Preston up and now stood somewhere behind him and was not in the circle. That woman took one end of the rope and circled her waist with it.

She turned in the other direction, and the woman on the other side of her helped her pull it around and tied it in a knot at her belly button, each woman using her one hand. Then the woman holding the coil of rope passed it around her own waist, and the woman who was already tied took it and helped her tie a similar knot. In this way they passed the rope around the circle, working together, tying themselves to each other. Jeez, is this what they teach over at Converse? Preston was about to ask, but he thought he better keep his mouth shut.

When the last woman was tied to the first, and the circle was complete, the priestess, who was still kneeling beside Preston and holding his hand again, not unkindly, began to sing a song he didn't recognize, something eerie like the hymn of female ghosts in a dilapidated mansion. The others joined in. Each woman raised her arm to the shoulder of the woman next to her, and they began to dance like the Greek kids at the Greek Festival—they hopped and dipped and skipped in their circle around the fire. Their bouncing jostled their hoods loose, and when Lynn's red hair burst free, it caught the blazing light of the fire and she seemed to be fire itself, pure energy, and Preston knew that she was precious and that he had to save her and that if he did, maybe she would save everyone.

He was just about to get up and run to her, sweep her into his arms and whisk her away—where?—maybe she was safest here—but then he remembered the arm bone—maybe he'd take her to his place—yes, oh yes—but the song and dance stopped, and the women picked up their knives. That gave him pause.

Each woman turned to her right and jabbed her knife into the empty sleeve of the woman beside her—I swan, Preston thought, I thought they were going to murder each other and cut each other's hearts out right there in front of my blurry eyes—but then they flicked knives back out, and lo and behold—arms. Every woman had two of them again, which they raised into the air in a gesture of victory as they whooped like warriors with scalps in their hands. The priestess took up her knife, handed it to him, lifted her empty sleeve with her free hand, showed him the thread that held it closed, and said, "Will you do me the honor, Mr. Earley?"

Darn right I will, Preston thought. He cut it, the sleeve opened, and her arm bloomed like a white rose from the fabric—she held out her hand for the knife. Reluctantly, he gave it back; she slid it into her belt and stood up.

"Stay right here," she ordered. "We're almost finished."

The priestess stepped into the circle, in front of the last woman to be tied, and untied the knot at the woman's waist. Then she took what looked like a gold coin out of her pocket and placed it in the woman's liberated hand with the benediction, "You are strong, rich, and free. Go proudly."

She kissed the woman on the forehead; the woman bowed and stepped back. The priestess proceeded, and one by one, reversing the order of the tying, she freed and paid her disciples. When the last was untied and the rope lay at their feet, they hugged each other and danced again, this time without shape or order. They frolicked like schoolgirls at a slumber party high on Cheez Whiz and Kool-Aid. But then Dennis brought over the real thing, two coolers of Michelob Light and Zima and boxes of souvlaki from the Sugar-n-Spice. Preston stood up, fixing to find Lynn—well, he didn't have to find her since he'd hardly taken his eyes off her during the whole show—but he lost his balance and fell—the drug, or whatever it was, obviously still had hold of him. Suddenly the priestess was kneeling at his side, propping him against the border stone.

"Sit still, Mr. Earley. We'll get you some food and drink, and you and I can talk." She signaled to one of the others.

"But I've got a murder to solve, dadgummit."

"Yes, the whole city is depending on you. We're trying to help. Haven't you learned a lot tonight?"

"Well, yeah, I guess you've tied up some of the loose ends."

"That's a clever pun, Mr. Earley."

"Call me Preston, please. What should I call you?"

"We don't use our names during the ceremony, at least we try not to."

"But that guy, what's his name—"

"Yes, well, he doesn't take our ritual as seriously as we do, but what can you expect? Call me Diana."

"Okay, Diana." One of the women brought over a skewer of souvlaki and a Michelob, and Preston thanked her, took a desperate swig of the cold beer. Then he turned back to Diana and asked, "Well, do you have any idea who the murderer is?"

"No, but you and I both know who the key is."

"Lynn. She's the connection between Phil Quake and Baxter Eerie."

Diana nodded. "That's what it looks like. I'm afraid she'll be next."

"Well, call her over. Maybe if the three of us put our heads together, we can make some sense of this thing."

"Maybe you're right." She stood up and walked away, leaving Preston to eat—the souvlaki wasn't as good as a Dionysus burger, but it was darn close.

But before he could chew down a single chunk of meat, Diana returned and said, “She’s gone.”

Chapter Eighteen

The sky was turning dull orange as they slowly descended from the foothills to the red, flat earth of Spartanburg. Preston drove slowly, even though the only traffic at this hour was from the shift change at the mills in Inman. The kid…what had "Diana" called him? Dennis?…was fidgeting next to him, which only made Preston's headache worse. "Calm down, now," he almost pleaded. "We'll get there."

"But my Mom'll kill me if she wakes up and I'm not there," Dennis whined, squeezing his knees with those shiny black fingernails. He remembered watching Dara—sweet, loving, comforting Dara—do her nails one time up at the boathouse, curled up in her favorite chair and wearing that shiny blue negligee that made him warm just to think about. Then he tried to imagine Dennis here, with the scraggly long hair and blotchy skin, doing *his* nails, dabbing away with that little brush soaked in black lacquer. His head throbbed even more at the thought. "Can't you drive any faster?" the kid whined again as they crawled past the big Baptist church at the northern edge of town.

Preston rubbed his aching temples, figured he might as well make the most of a nervous, captive suspect, and dived right in. "What the heck are you doing out there with those women?" he blurted out.

"They're just a bunch of crazy ol' ladies," Dennis said. "They don't mean no trouble to nobody."

Preston thought of Lynn. Not crazy, no. And definitely not old. He expected even Dennis had noticed that fact. "They pay you to help out?"

"Thirty bucks to help 'em lug that stupid column, carry their bags of stuff. Easy money. And once a month, to boot."

"And that was Peggy Sue Eerie, wasn't it. That's what you called her when she was waving that knife at me."

"I ain't sayin'."

"C'mon, Dennis. You go out there every month because of Lynn, right? Baxter Eerie's daughter, the one with the red hair. You like being near her, don't you."

"You're as crazy as they are!" Dennis protested. "You leave her out of this!"

Ah. A raw nerve. "In fact," he carried on in pursuit, "I think you'd do anything she asked you to. Like steal an audiotape." He noticed the black nails dig even deeper as Dennis turned away and stared out the window, sullen and silent, the hiss of tires against damp pavement filling the car. The USCS campus, then the Milliken Research Center had glided by before another idea struggled to light.

"What was that she said?" he asked out loud. "Something about rebirth..."

"I wasn't payin' attention," Dennis mumbled.

With a start, Preston saw the butcher knife again, gleaming in the firelight. *It's not about death, Mr. Earley. It's about rebirth.* That's what Peggy Sue had said, wasn't it? And why did that seem important? Rebirth...

"Church Street," Dennis suddenly said.

"What?"

"I live on Church Street."

Preston knew which house it was even before Dennis pointed it out. It was the house with the purple Volkswagen parked in the front yard. He grabbed an arm before Dennis could scramble out of the car. "Yeah, I reckon you'd do anything she asked you to. Even running someone off the road to put him out of commission for awhile."

He felt the surrender, Dennis' arm going slack in his grip. "She was tryin' to protect you," he said. "'Out of harm's way,' that's what she said."

Scare him off, more like it. And it had almost worked, if poor Chester hadn't spilled the beans about the border stone. He let Dennis go. "Go on, now. And have a good breakfast before you go to school. Most important meal of the day, y'know." Dennis scooted away, disappearing around the back of the darkened house just as the sun began to peek over the towers of Spartanburg Regional. Another day being born…

Born. Born again. Reborn. Rebirth…Something that had been thought lost, appearing again. The rebirth of lost knowledge, like when Miss Feeney in high school used to talk about the Renaissance…

Preston slammed his foot to the floor, no doubt waking up Dennis' mother with the squeal of rubber as he sped away toward Daniel Morgan Avenue, toward the red gash where Spartanburg's downtown was supposed to be reborn. The Renaissance Project. Dara had even mentioned it once, but he had chalked it up to her habit of trusting intuition and not cold, hard facts. "Men think they *know* things," she'd told him once. "But women *feel* things. That's why guys used to go to all those Muses and Oracles to figure things out. That's why men fall for women. 'Cause they want the inside story before the other guy figures it out."

Out his passenger-side window, he just caught a glimpse of the startled figure—a strangely familiar figure, broad-shouldered, long-legged, agile—that jumped to its feet and dashed away into the shadows. But what Preston feared, what brought a low moan to his lips as he scrambled over the piles of concrete and splintering timber, was the other figure lying motionless on the ground. Red hair, and something else red, soaking a light-colored shirt. Preston knew now that Lynn had tried to save him once by stashing him safely away in a hospital bed. He prayed hard that he'd be able to return the favor.

Chapter Nineteen

The siren began, a distant whisper of confirmation that what he was seeing was true. He'd had the presence of mind to call 911, but he was still hoping to awaken, or to somehow be shaken from this terrible vision.

Lynn lay below him, bleeding and unconscious. He shed his shirt and placed it over the deep knife wound in her stomach. Something on the ground beside them startled him. It looked to be a playing card, but when he picked it up, he saw that it was a Tarot card. Not just any Tarot card, but the Death card.

Geez, he thought. In an instant he saw that the real killer's attempts to cast off suspicion had reached a point so lame as to be almost laughable. He pocketed the card. Tampering with evidence was nothing new to him, and he figured he'd be serving justice anyway, since some fool investigator might actually be misled by the stupid planted clue.

The siren's crescendo broke his heart, bringing him back to reality. He couldn't bear to look at her anymore, so he turned, keeping his hand and shirt over her wound. He stared over his shoulder toward town, where the sun was just beginning to bathe the Morgan statue in the square, casting just a hint of a shadow, which seemed, in some odd way, to shape a truth not yet clear to Preston. He hoped the truth would come to full light soon.

The ambulance pulled up and its flashing light broke his field of vision, casting measured rounds of redness. He lifted his hand and stood, leaving Lynn to God and the professionals, not knowing at the moment how much he trusted either. He watched the paramedics load her body into the ambulance.

A car door slammed and Jake raced toward Preston.

"Where's Bo?" he asked.

"I don't know," Preston replied.

* * *

In the waiting room outside the ER at Spartanburg Regional, Preston paced the floor. Though his mind was mostly occupied with worry for Lynn, who'd been back in the ER for close to an hour, the important questions kept resurfacing through the worry.

Who? Why? Renaissance Project?

Frank and other various Eeries huddled in one corner of the waiting room, sobbing and hugging, patting each other's hands and passing Kleenexes. Frank eyed another corner of the room with contempt, the corner where Lynn's women friends formed a circle and held hands, sobbing and whispering things about healing and renewal.

The door to the outside swung open and Bo Hunter walked in.

"Arrest those women, Bo!" Frank yelled.

Preston stopped his pacing just in front of Bo.

"How is she?" Bo asked.

"Don't know," said Preston. "They won't let me back there and they won't tell me a thing. What's the word on the crime scene investigation?"

"Well, by the time they tracked me down and I got there, Jake and his boys had already had a forensics feast, so I didn't stay. I came straight here to see how she's doing." He motioned toward the women in the corner, dropped his voice to a whisper. "I guess Lynn must've done something to tick off some of those witchy friends of hers. I can't believe they have the gall to be here. As soon as my backups get here, we're turning the heat up a notch on their little Satanic butts."

Frank had moved close enough to hear Bo say this and he nodded emphatically.

"What makes you so sure they're responsible?" Preston said.

"Oh, my God, Earley!" Frank said in a whisper loud enough to attract stares from the women. He dropped his voice a little. "Wake up and smell the eye of newt in the room. Of course those broom riders are responsible!"

Bo continued in a quiet, calm tone. "It just makes sense, Preston. All the weird cult stuff associated with the whole thing, starting with Quake and all that furniture piled up, and now that creepy Death card beside this victim's body…"

The door from the ER burst open, interrupting them.

"Doc!" Preston said. "How is she?"

"We think she's going to be okay. The damage to her organs was much less severe than we expected. She lost a lot of blood, and her type is not common, but luckily the Blood Bank had an adequate supply."

The whole crowd from all corners quickly congregated around the doctor. Frank Eerie shoved his way to the front.

"Is she conscious?" he said. "Can we see her?"

"Not right now. She's resting and she doesn't need any visitors whatsoever."

Bo flashed his badge.

"I *really* need to talk to her," he said.

Preston looked at Bo, recalling what he'd said before the doctor had burst into the room. He wondered how Bo knew about the Tarot card. Nobody had seen that but him. Was Bo Hunter a supercop, or what?

Preston grabbed Bo's arm.

"Can I talk to you in private, Detective?" Preston said.

"Not now, Earley," Bo said, trying to follow the doctor back through the door to the ER.

Preston grabbed his arm more forcefully and pulled him around to face him.

"Are you sure it was the Death card you saw at the crime scene?" He stared hard at Bo. "'Cause, you know, I think maybe it was the Judgment card."

"Judgment card?"

"Yeah, the Judgment card. At least that's the card that *should've* been there."

Bo still stared. Lynn's friends formed a circle around the men. Frank was caught in the circle with them.

"See," Preston continued, "Dara used to fool with those cards some, so I know a little. And I happen to remember that the Judgment card can stand for rebirth."

"Rebirth," Bo, repeated, looking quizzically at Preston.

"What in the name of Lucifer are you talking about, Earley?" Frank said.

The women tightened their circle around the three men. Outside their circle, Lynn's other relatives clustered and listened.

"Rebirth," said Preston, "as in Renaissance. As in Renaissance Project."

Preston and Bo stared hard at each other. Frank stood beside them, redfaced and shaking a little.

"Tell me what you know, Bo," said Preston.

"I don't like your tone, Earley," Bo replied.

Chapter Twenty

BY MEG BARNHOUSE

The door from the ER swung open fast, and a woman burst into the room. Her face was set, furious. Preston recognized her—she was the one-armed woman from Peggy Sue's kitchen shop. Quickly scanning the room, she found Bo and called to him in a voice harsh with emotion. "Officer! I have some things to tell you!" As she spoke, she brushed aside Lynn's milling women friends and family members until she reached him. Preston could feel the heat from her body as she stood looking from him to Bo, breathing hard, her high cheekbones flushed with color.

"It's over now. They hurt my daughter, and it's over. I can't sit back and watch them do this anymore. It has to stop."

"Ma'am, please try to calm down." Bo put his

hand on her arm. She shook him off.

"Calm down? You ask me to calm down when my daughter lies in there with her stomach bleeding?" She looked at Preston as if to enlist his help in this outrageous situation.

Preston said, "Maybe we can find a room where we can talk."

"My car's right out front," Bo said. "We need to go down to the station if you have a statement to make." He looked at the woman. All eyes in the room were on the three of them. Frank's mouth was open in a perfect O. "Can you leave your daughter for a short time, Ms....?"

"If we're not gone too long. And it's Furia. Trixie Furia. Lynn Eerie's mother."

So this beauty with the face and body of a Greek sculpture was the woman Baxter met at the Marshall Tucker concert twenty years ago. Baxter had said on the phone that she was living in Florida somewhere. Preston wanted to think, but there was no time, as Ms. Furia began talking again as soon as she was ensconced in the front seat of the Lieutenant's Crown Vic, with Preston in the back, and the blinker pointing left toward Church Street.

"I came up from Florida last year to be near Lynn—I didn't know how she would handle the stress of being away from home, and in the middle of the Eeries. She's not a bad girl, just easily misled. I wasn't going to come, but as soon as she got up here, there was a tone in her voice—it reminded me of how she sounded right before I had to put her in the hospital in the tenth grade. I got worried about her, and Peggy Sue was kind enough to give me a job, and then when I lost my arm to the cancer this summer, she and her women's group were so kind to me, even doing that funeral for my arm up there at the border stone. Lynn got interested in trauma during my illness, but I think the surgery may have rattled her a bit more than it should have. I know I'm babbling, and I'm sorry. I'm just so upset."

Bo drove in silence, turning onto Church Street. Preston said, "Just tell us about what's going on, Trixie." He tried to make his voice calming and kind. His heart was pounding, and all the colors of the night looked unnaturally bright. Adrenaline. Or was it love?

"A couple of weeks ago, Lynn found out her Uncle Frank had set her up to take the blame for—well, after she had been trying to help him."

"Help him?" Bo asked.

"He asked her to—uh—romance Phil Quake a little. Frank thought he could be so helpful in his project, you know, the Renaissance, with the influence he had on public opinion in this town, and if Lynn were friendly with him she could, you know, feed him information about the project, as an insider. She wasn't actually sleeping with him, I'm sure, she wasn't that ruthless a girl…" her voice trailed off uncertainly.

Her shoulders squared as she found her focus again. "What I wanted to tell you, is that I think Frank was behind Phil Quake's murder!"

Bo flipped his left blinker on and turned down Daniel Morgan, toward Pine Street. Away from the police station. Bo shifted in his seat. Preston's chest seized. He had a very bad feeling. "Where are you going? I thought we were…" his throat squeezed too tight for talking as he saw the gleam along the barrel of the .38 in Bo's hand. His mind went blank as a chalkboard before class. It would be nice if some instructions would appear, neatly lettered by the Cosmic Teacher. Nothing. He could reach for Bo's throat, but Bo would shoot him dead in a New York minute. He had seen Bo in action in 'Nam. Bo didn't have a sweet heap of human feeling.

Preston thought about his own gun, stuck deep into a canister of ground coffee to keep it rust-free. He got his Blue Ridge Blend at The Sandwich Factory, sometimes at Java Jive if he was feeling hip. The lamps there sometimes had bizarre things to say to him if he'd been off his meds. He mentally shook himself and tried to focus. No gun. Think. Threads of the story tangled in his mind as if ten deranged voices were shouting clues at him all at the same time. Trixie Furia gaped at the gun for a moment, temporarily silent. Then she shut her mouth and looked like she was thinking hard.

So Frank had tried to set Lynn up. Preston remembered the note from her to Phil, written in a handwriting that was different from the writing on her photograph in Phil's pocket. Faked.

Lynn was helping Frank at first. That's why she tried to hypnotize him at the hospital. The car jerked across Pine Street and onto Isom. The empty Beaumont Mill loomed on the right. And Bo. His old buddy. His recent suspicions had been on target. The figure Preston had seen sloping off into the shadows near the wounded Lynn, his knowing which Tarot card was at the scene. How could he have known?

"The card," he said out loud to Bo. "You were the one who knifed Lynn."

"Don't be ridiculous. The uniforms who took your call radioed me with details."

"Ms. Furia, please continue. I need to hear what you have to say."

"You were the one who hurt my daughter!" Her hand was in a fist, her teeth bared. Preston didn't know whether she would ignore the gun and attack Bo. Bo lifted the gun and pointed it at her sideways, keeping his eye on the road.

"Your daughter is a piece of work, ma'am. I'm sure you know that. She didn't turn a hair when she found out that the meet she had lured Quake to so she could 'give him information' about Renaissance was in fact so we could get him out of the way. He'd been working on a big story, about to blow the whistle on the whole thing—something about the money from the state, I didn't follow the whole thing. Mr. E. told me it would be very detrimental to our project, so I got him out of the way."

"Just to help out?" Preston asked, dryly.

"Listen, I'm going to be the Big Dog when this thing goes through. Do you have any idea how tired I am of this podunk town where nothing ever changes? Mr. E. has big plans for this place." They were traveling along the railroad tracks. Ike's flashed by. Preston thought of the great chili cheeseburgers there. Mustard and slaw. He wanted more than he could say to stay alive to eat another one.

"She's just troubled." Trixie was focused on her daughter. "You know that runs in the Eerie side. Her Aunt Lucille had some of those same troubles, but she has made a good life for herself teaching algebra. And she has been such a help to Lynn through my illness. I have to admit that I didn't want the two of them to have a lot of contact, being so much alike. Lucille scares me sometimes…"

"So Lynn knew you killed Phil Quake." Preston said it to see how it flew.

"She didn't care. Just laughed when I told her I'd piled the furniture on him like there was going to be a fire, after I cut out his heart. Those crazy women are going down for this. They don't stand a chance. Ceremonial rituals in Spartanburg? The people will tear them limb from limb. Sermons will be preached. It'll clean up the town and get the project back on track."

"That's why you sent me on that wild goose chase after the cooking school interview tape—to throw suspicion on Peggy Sue and her group."

Bo chuckled. "You went for that one, bro. Then Dara told me you'd been having flashbacks to the time when she took you out there with her to one of the meetings. Left you in the car. You were having a rough time, you know, with your little voices, and you'd been to Rockers. She thought you were sleeping in the car, but I guess you must've opened your eyes once or twice. Said she got bored with it and never went back. She was worried about you. Nice girl. Drinks too much, but..." Dara. Preston wondered what she was doing right now. Trixie looked at him with those large and ancient eyes. Her sensual mouth made Dara's picture fade. He was going to save this woman. Save her, then kiss her. Yeah.

"Why Chester, Bo? May as well tell me, since it seems you're going to kill us. Did he see you?"

"Nah, he was just unreliable. For a while, he was funneling you all the information I would tell him to, but he wasn't the steadiest. I thought he was too dumb to figure the whole thing out, but when I saw him try to talk to Lynn and Lucille at Baxter's funeral, I knew he needed to go." They had crossed Skylyn and turned past Hardee's, right onto East Main.

"You better hope you've got the keys to Peggy Sue's shop, Miss Trixie. We got to get us a plan."

"Two more bodies in that sweet woman's lap, huh, Lieutenant?" Trixie had grasped the situation. "If she goes down, won't that hurt Frank? Won't that hurt the Renaissance Project?"

"Doesn't Frank know Peggy Sue's in that group, Bo? Doesn't he care?"

"He's ready to be done with her, man. Plus the sympathy alone will give him the public support he needs."

They had braked at the curb in front of the cooking store. Pairs and clusters of the young and chic were milling around Gerhardt's. Preston tried to think of a way to catch their attention. Blank again.

The store was dark. Bo gestured with the gun toward the back of the store, and grunted that they should sit at the marble-topped counter. He shoved a candle at Trixie and a packet of matches, and told her to light it. The copper pots and utensils gleamed red in the light of the flame.

Trixie's eyes flashed. "You're not going to get away with this! Lynn told me everything when she figured out she was being set up to take the blame for everything. She was so hurt when they moved that old house and there were her pictures and tapes under there, no doubt with her fingerprints all over them!"

"Were they her—uh—hands, too, Trixie?" Preston had to know. The hands in the Sugar-n-Spice to-go box had been too weird. Trixie looked uncomfortable.

"Well, the trouble we had in Florida when Lynn

was in high school, she was working at the hospital, as a candy striper, you know, I thought it would be good for her, get her out of herself a little, anyway, it turned out she'd begun—removing items from the premises. We got her help! That was a long time ago, and I can't believe Frank would use that knowledge to set up his own niece! And so far in advance!"

"Insurance," Bo said, curtly, "Just in case things got rough. Frank told me to get that Dennis kid who was working with us to pick up some hands from his job at the morgue." Preston shook his head. Dennis was working for everybody. "Frank wanted a fall guy," Bo continued. "Who better than his little crazy niece?"

"I still don't get it, Bo." Preston was thinking fast. He wished the general were closer so he could get some more advice. "You were right there with me when you found out Lynn's dad, Baxter, was coming in to the station. I called him from the library and didn't tell you until he was due to come in. Then he showed up dead in the back of Belk dorm."

"That stumped me, too, Preston," Bo said. "Baxter wasn't any part of this."

"Maybe Frank was more hands-on in this thing than you knew," Preston guessed. "Maybe you blackmailed him into killing Baxter so you wouldn't be hanging out there all on your own in case things went bad. So you'd have something on him, too."

A voice came from the front of the store. "Frank

wouldn't have the guts to kill anyone, would he, Bo?"
Bo whipped around toward the voice, which demanded icily, "Drop your gun." Preston felt Trixie jump with a jerk. Bo's gun clattered to the floor.

"I had Frank Eerie in my first algebra class." Lucille Stone moved forward, into the circle of the candle's light. "I've known him thirty years, and he doesn't have what it takes. Ambitious, yes, but he doesn't have the soldier's heart. Calls himself a Spartan." The stern-faced woman snorted derisively. "It was I who ended Baxter's life. He was going to put Lynn away again. That's what she was worried about when she called me after he phoned her at school to ask her why he was being called to the police station.

"She is the closest thing I have in the world to a daughter. That girl has a soldier's heart, uncorrupted with giggling sentimentality. I couldn't let him shut her away from the light of the sun with a gaggle of lunatics! I killed him. She will get over the loss. It's better this…"

"You're crazy!" Trixie shouted.

"No. You see, there is no proof Lynn was involved in any of this. It suits me for those New Age Maenads to take the blame for everything. Bo is right. They didn't listen to me when I tried to tell them about real Dionysian rites, rites built around real sacrifice. They told me they were 'uncomfortable' with my views and asked me to leave the group." She laughed unpleasantly, and focused on Bo.

"Did you know that, up through the Middle Ages and the Renaissance, even into the nineteenth century, people understood that there had to be bodies in the foundation to make a strong building? Spiritually strong, that is. For this Renaissance, that will benefit us all so greatly, there must be a sacrifice. Three more to make the city strong again, I think. You first," she said to Bo, "since you stabbed my dear niece." She fired twice. The sound was deafening in the enclosed shop. Bo's shriek echoed off the copper ware as he slumped heavily to the floor. Preston felt Trixie move behind him, and he turned to pull her onto the floor behind the counter. Surely someone had heard the shots, and they would come running. Trixie swore as he pulled her to the floor, and she shoved him away from her and tried to stand up.

"NO! Stay down!"

"Let me up, fool!" Trixie hissed. There was another loud thump, as if another body had hit the floor. Preston peeked around the counter, and saw Lucille lying in a heap, the handle of a large kitchen knife protruding from her chest. He stared at Trixie, who had grabbed another knife and was stepping gingerly toward Lucille. She crouched by her and felt for her pulse.

"Not dead, but dying," she said, in a flat voice.

"You threw that knife?"

"Yeah, as she shot Bo. Too bad it was too late for him." She didn't sound like she thought it was too bad.

"Where did you learn to do that?" Preston asked, astonished.

Trixie Furia straightened up, and shrugged. "Business has been a little slow lately."

Epilogue

Lynn recovered, and was given into the care of a competent therapist as she continued at Converse. Preston and Trixie dated for a while, but it never really went anywhere. Dara called after a few months, and Preston and she resumed their dance.

Frank disavowed any knowledge of what Bo had been doing. He and Peggy Sue decided they loved each other right much, and they had a ceremony of renewal of their vows at the Episcopal Church. No one ever understood what was happening with the Renaissance Project.

Biographies

John Lane is a poet, essayist, editor and fiction writer. He teaches English and creative writing at Wofford College and is a three-time winner of the South Carolina Fiction Project.

Pat Jobe is one of the authors of *Radio Free Bubba.* His commentaries are featured on WNCW public radio, in ten regional newspapers and on the CD *Sex and Ice Cream.* His new novel, *365 Ways to Criticize the Preacher*, will be published in 2002.

Rob Brown, a native of Spartanburg, was published recently in a serial novel in *Southerner* online magazine. Another article of his will appear in an upcoming issue of *Outdoor Life.*

Susan Beckham Jackson teaches English and creative writing at Spartanburg Technical College. One of her stories appears in Hub City's 2001 release, *Inheritance: Selections from the South Carolina Fiction Project.*

Thomas McConnell teaches creative writing at the University of South Carolina Spartanburg and was the winner of the 2000 Hub City Hardegree Prize in Short Fiction. His stories have appeared in magazines in Atlanta and New York.

Rosa Shand is the author of *The Gravity of Sunlight*, published by Soho Press in April 2000, and is a five-time winner of the South Carolina Fiction Project. She is the recipient of an NEA Fellowship in Fiction.

Deno Trakas teaches English at Wofford College and is a four-time winner of the South Carolina Fiction Project. Three of his stories are published in Hub City's *New Southern Harmonies.*

Norman Powers, who lives in Landrum, had a twenty-year career in television and film production in New York City. He won Hub City's Hardegree Prize in Creative Nonfiction in 1999.

Sam Howie is a social worker in Gaffney and a graduate student of writing at Vermont College. His work is published in *Hub City Christmas*.

Meg Barnhouse is the author of *Rock of Ages at the Taj Mahal*. Her work has been published in four Hub City books, including *The Best of Radio Free Bubba*.

Colophon

In Morgan's Shadow was designed during a three-week break in one of the South's most bone-chilling, record-breaking, power-consuming winters to date. *Updating* the previous technology update, February 2001: This *REALLY IS* the last Hub City project to be "processed" on the trio of original (and still reliable) 1992 Power Macintosh© 7100/80s. The two speedier, beige desktop G3s are waiting on the floor to be configured. The faster, 300mhz machine is packing 256 meg of ram, a speedy Yamaha© CD burner, Mac OS 9.0.1, Pagemaker© 6.5 *Plus,* Photoshop© 6.0, an internal Zip© drive and a 45 gig hard drive. WOW! The 233mhz G3 is *not* far behind. This twelfth HCWP title is released in a first printing of 1500 soft-bound. The text typeface is AGaramond and the display face is Schmutz ICG Corroded. Recycle Reverse is used for the authors' names, while Schmutz ICG Corroded adds a finishing touch to the drop caps. The "magic" of Guinness© Draught greatly relieved the brain-strain of long production hours.

The Hub City Writers Project is a non-profit organization whose mission is to foster a sense of community through the literary arts. We do this by publishing books from and about our community; encouraging, mentoring, and advancing the careers of local writers; and seeking to make Spartanburg a center for the literary arts.

Our metaphor of organization purposely looks backward to the nineteenth century when Spartanburg was known as the "hub city," a place where railroads converged and departed.

At the beginning of the twenty-first century, Spartanburg has become a literary hub of South Carolina with an active and nationally celebrated core group of poets, fiction writers, and essayists. We celebrate these writers—and the ones not yet discovered—as one of our community's greatest assets. William R. Ferris, former director of the Center for the Study of Southern Cultures, says of the emerging South, "Our culture is our greatest resource. We can shape an economic base...And it won't be an investment that will disappear."

Hub City Anthology • John Lane & Betsy Teter, editors
Hub City Music Makers • Peter Cooper
Hub City Christmas • John Lane & Betsy Wakefield Teter, editors
New Southern Harmonies • Rosa Shand, Scott Gould, Deno Trakas, George Singleton
The Best of Radio Free Bubba • Meg Barnhouse, Pat Jobe, Kim Taylor, Gary Phillips
Family Trees: The Peach Culture of the Piedmont • Mike Corbin
Seeing Spartanburg: A History in Images • Philip Racine
The Seasons of Harold Hatcher • Mike Hembree
The Lawson's Fork: Headwaters to Confluence • David Taylor, Gary Henderson
Hub City Anthology 2 • Betsy Wakefield Teter, editor
Inheritance • Janette Turner Hospital, editor

"Enjoy your muffins, Chester."
"Two big blueberry muffins," Chester said, spinning toward The Sandwich Factory.

—Preston Earley and Crazy Chester
conversing on Morgan Square
(chapter 1)

"No one makes yeast rolls like Wade's."

—Preston Earley to Jake the Snake
(chapter 13)

"You've heard of the Mediterranean diet, haven't you? All Greek food is healthy."

—Theo, proprietor of Sugar-n-Spice,
to Preston Earley *(chapter 7)*

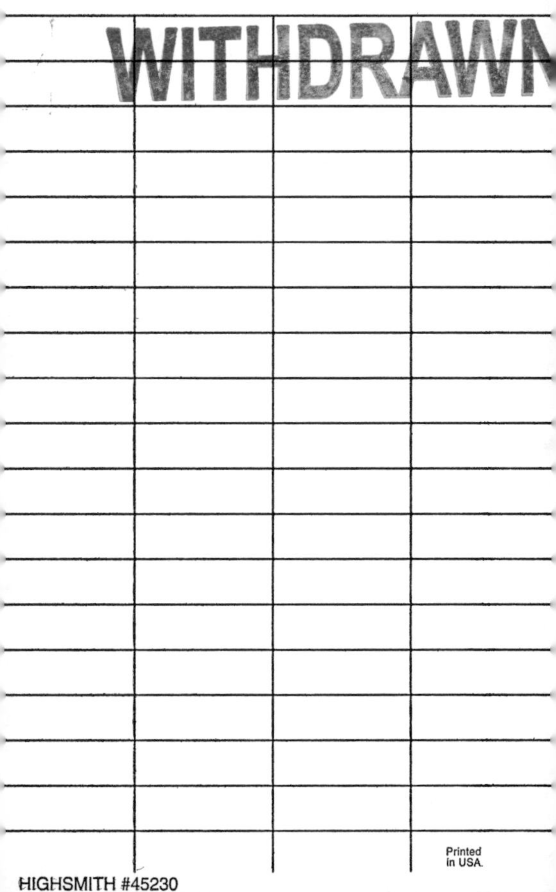
WITHDRAWN
Printed in USA.